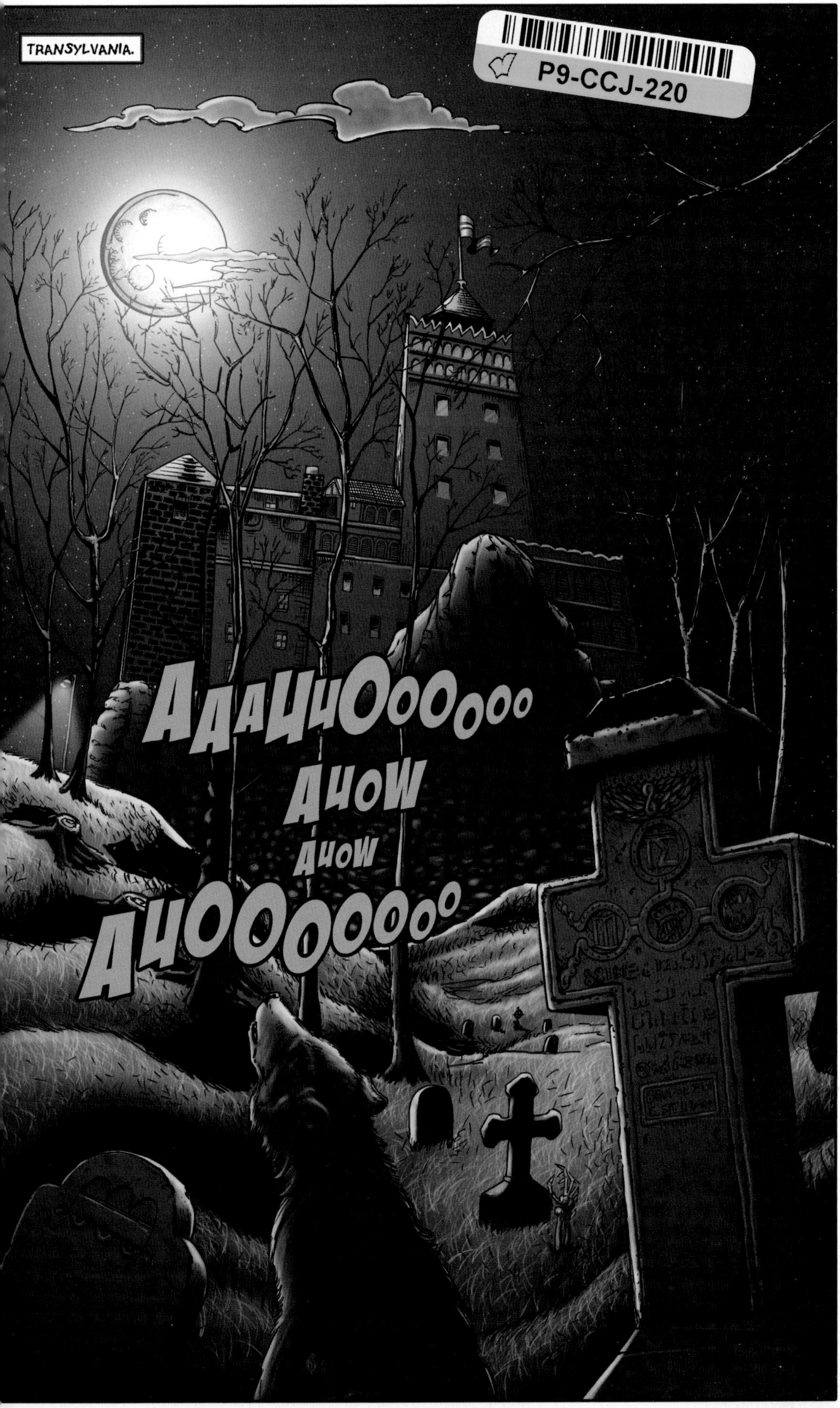
TRANSYLVANIA.
AAAUUOOOOooo
AUOW
AUOW
AUOOOOOOo

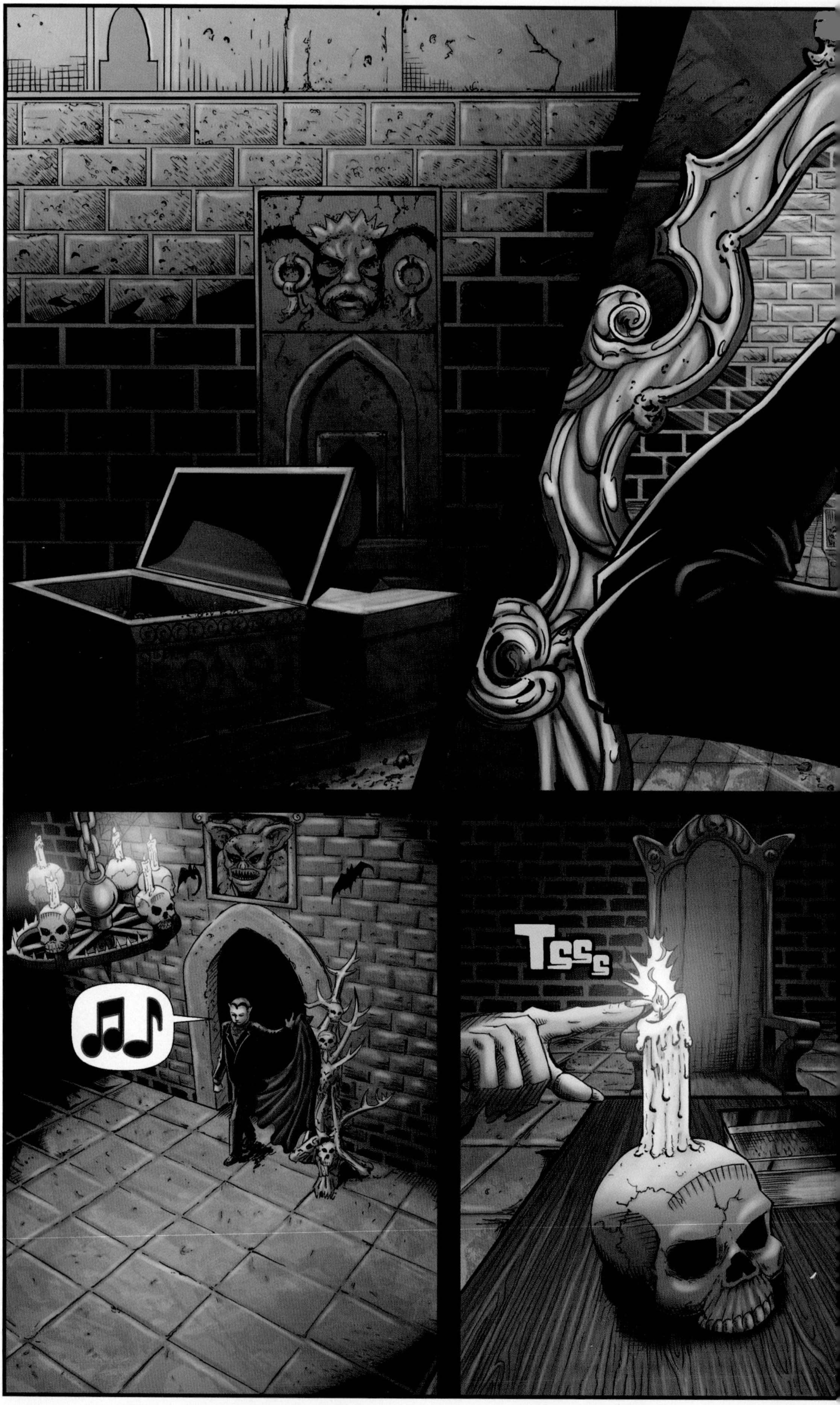
Tsss

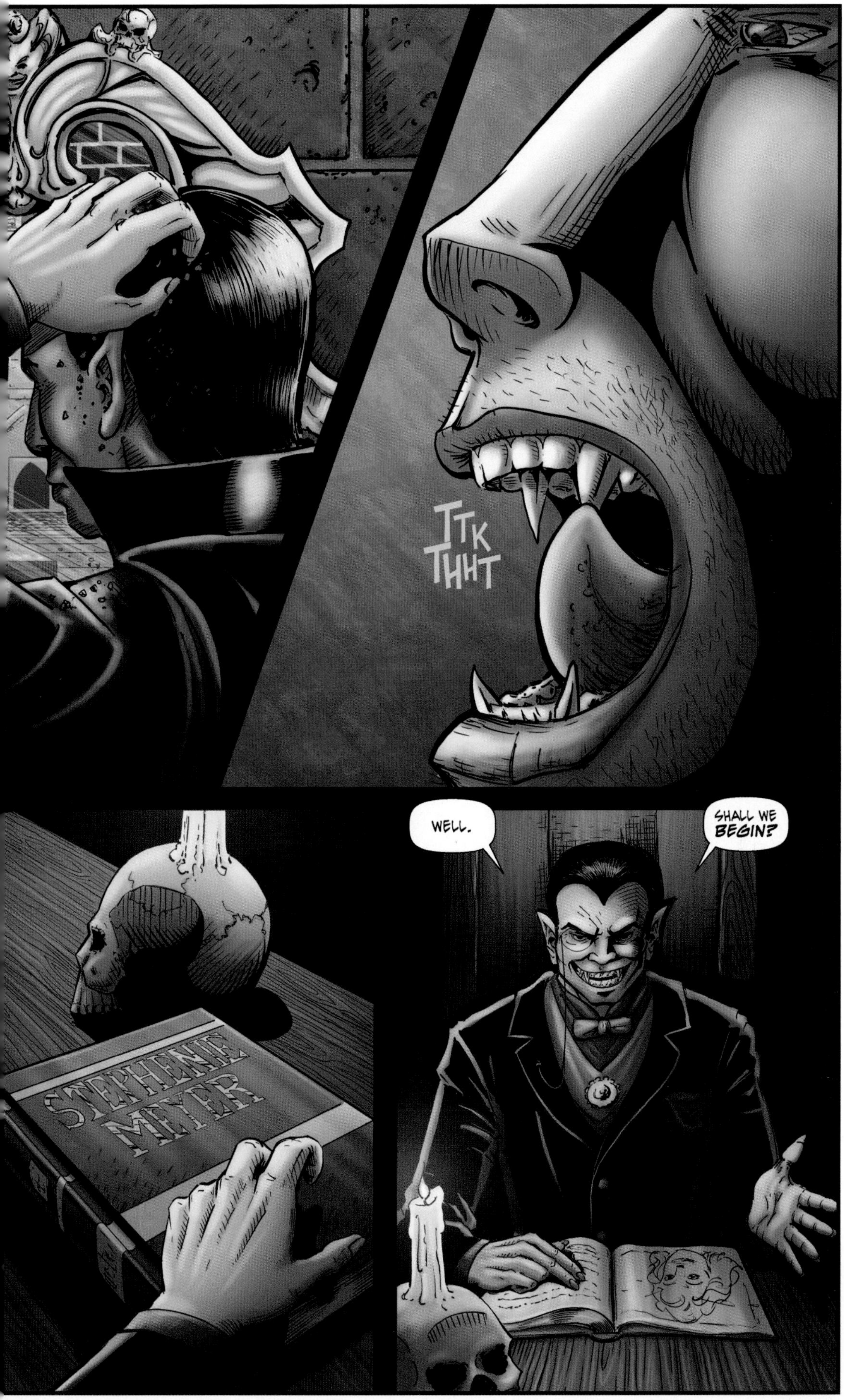
TTK THHT
WELL.
SHALL WE BEGIN?
STEPHENIE MEYER

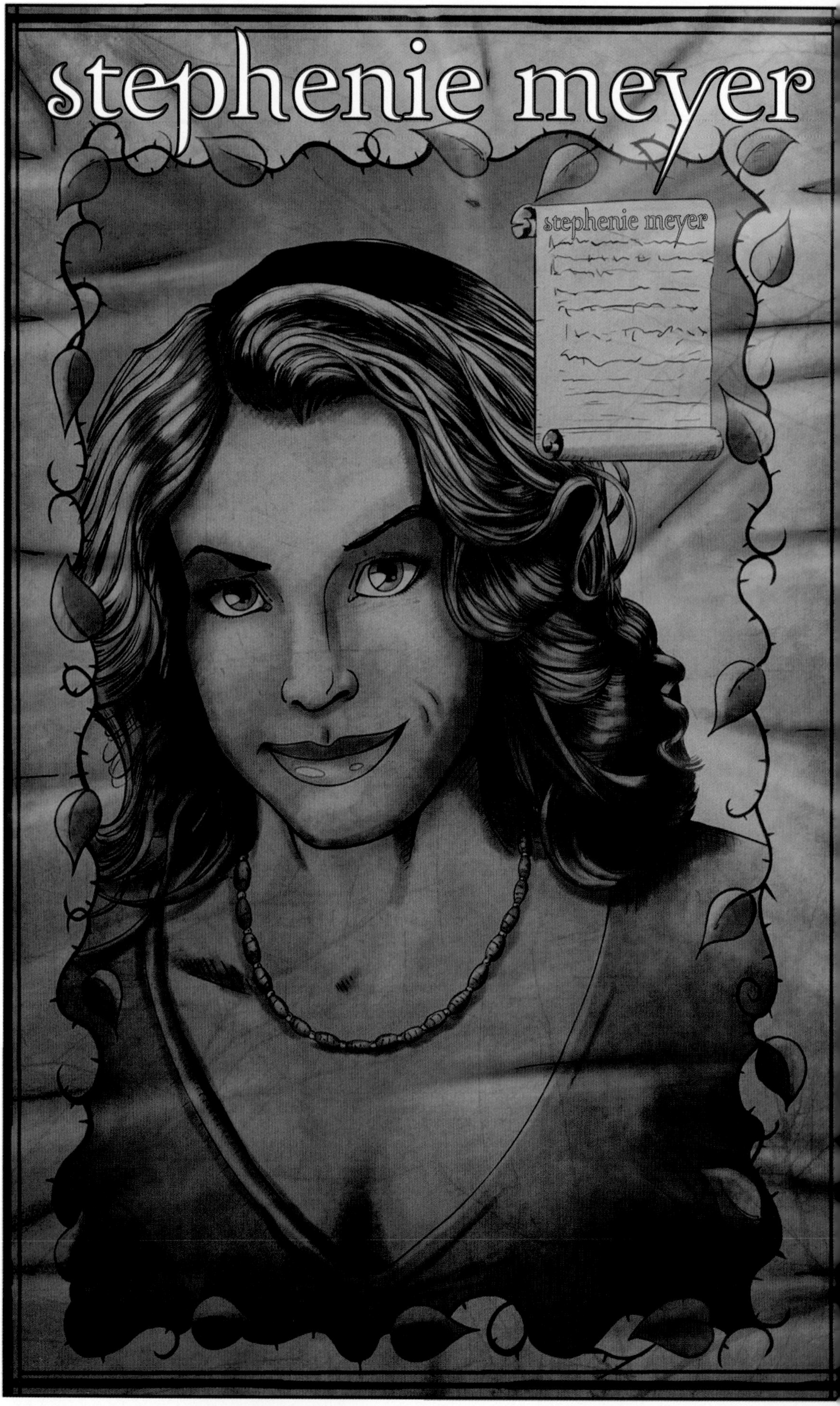
stephenie meyer
stephenie meyer

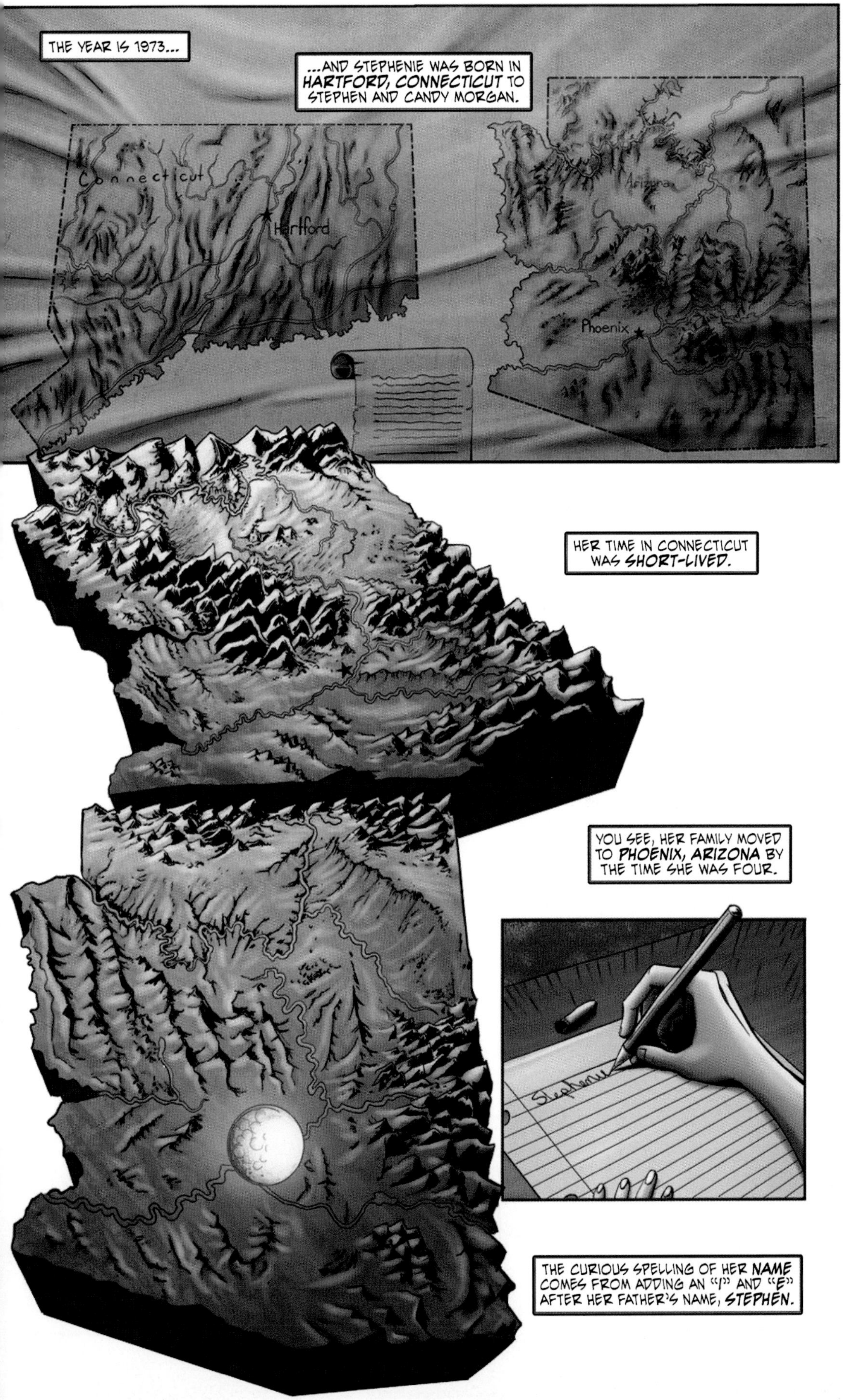
THE YEAR IS 1973...
...AND STEPHENIE WAS BORN IN HARTFORD, CONNECTICUT TO STEPHEN AND CANDY MORGAN.
Connecticut
Hartford
Arizona
Phoenix
HER TIME IN CONNECTICUT WAS SHORT-LIVED.
YOU SEE, HER FAMILY MOVED TO PHOENIX, ARIZONA BY THE TIME SHE WAS FOUR.
THE CURIOUS SPELLING OF HER NAME COMES FROM ADDING AN "I" AND "E" AFTER HER FATHER'S NAME, STEPHEN.

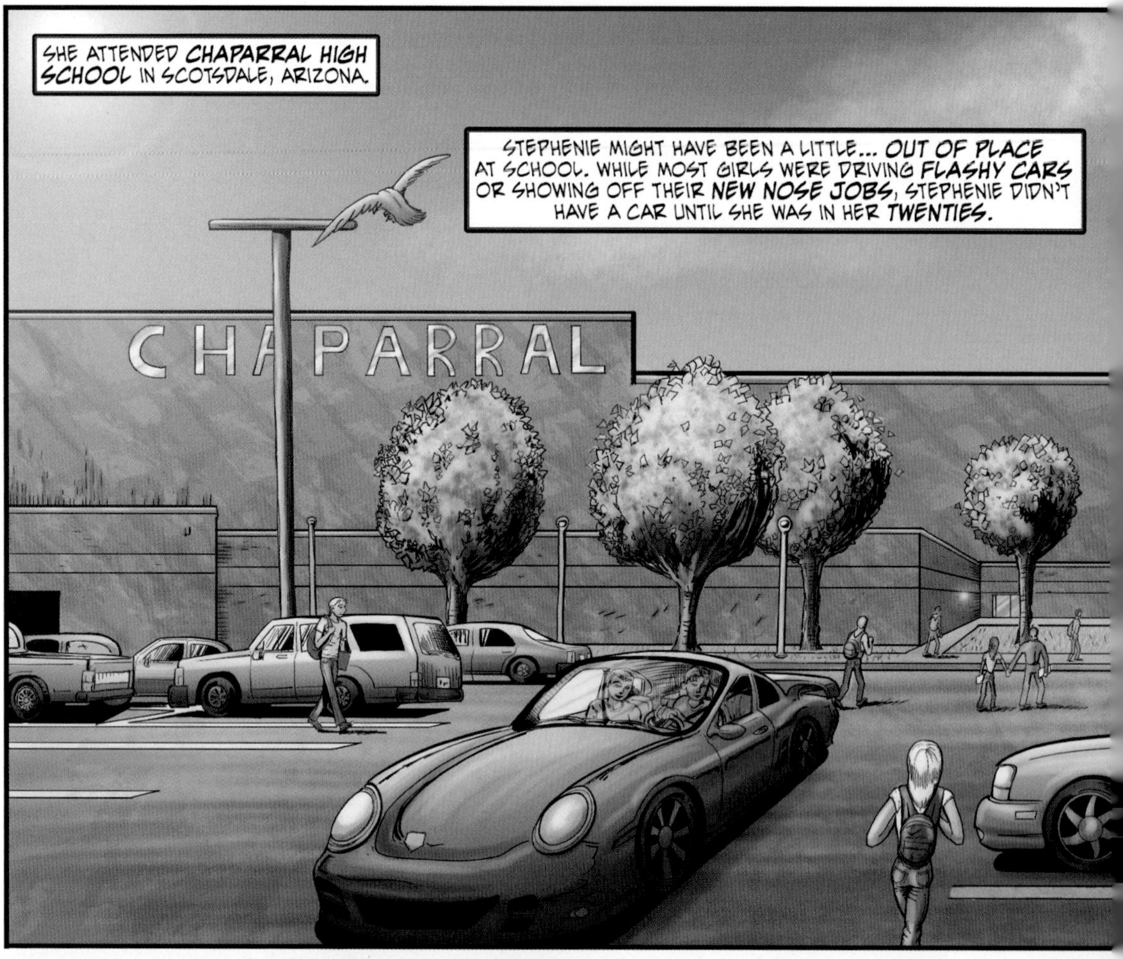
SHE ATTENDED CHAPARRAL HIGH SCHOOL IN SCOTSDALE, ARIZONA.
STEPHENIE MIGHT HAVE BEEN A LITTLE... OUT OF PLACE AT SCHOOL. WHILE MOST GIRLS WERE DRIVING FLASHY CARS OR SHOWING OFF THEIR NEW NOSE JOBS, STEPHENIE DIDN'T HAVE A CAR UNTIL SHE WAS IN HER TWENTIES.
CHAPARRAL

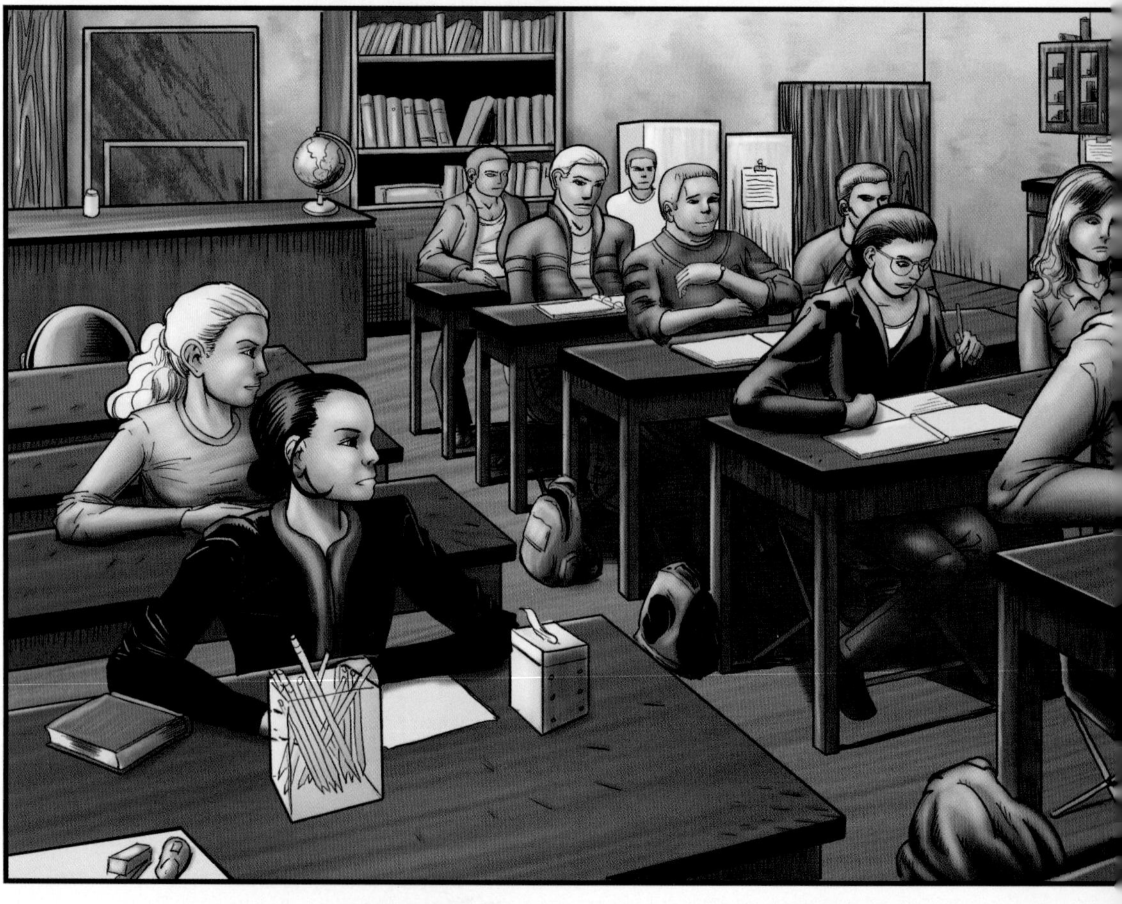

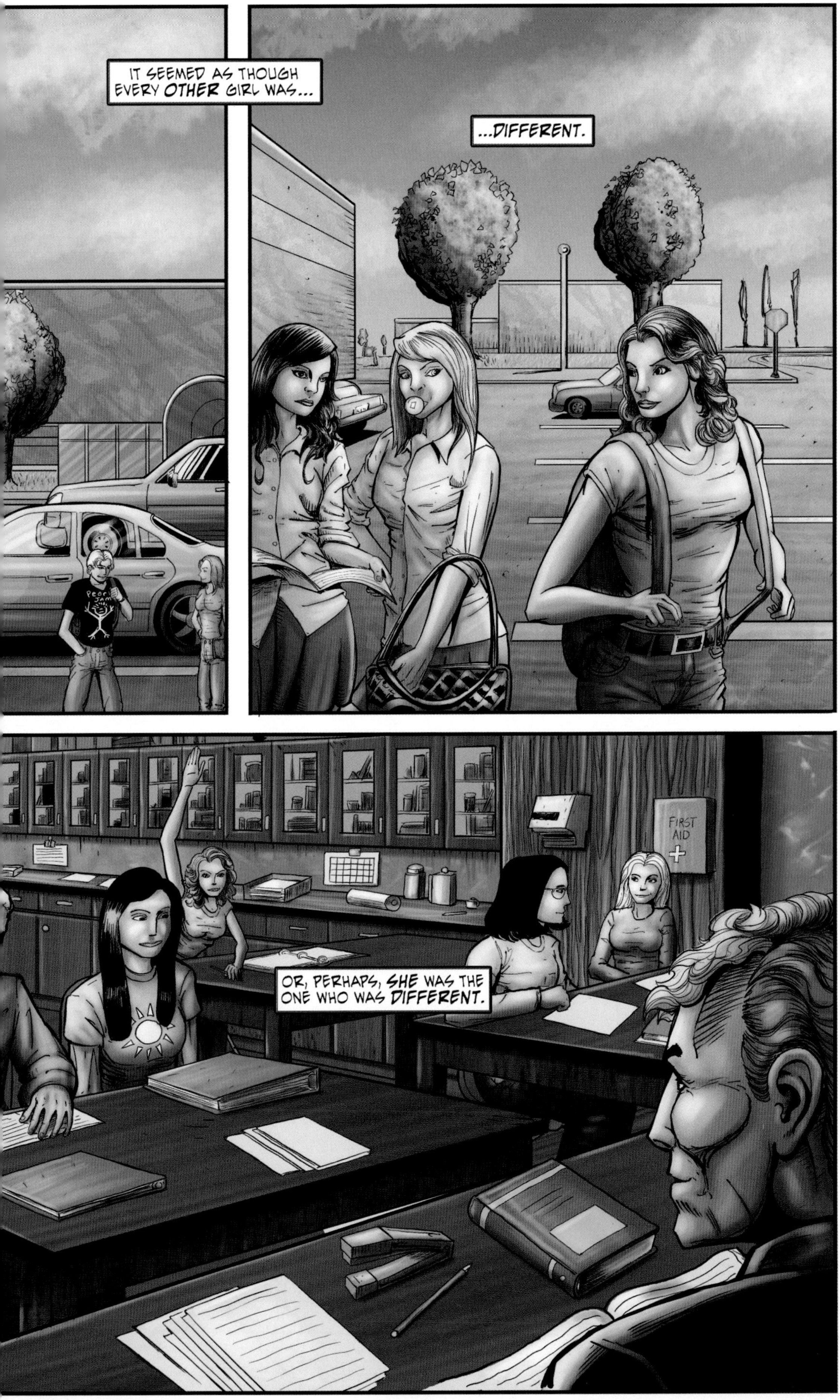
IT SEEMED AS THOUGH EVERY OTHER GIRL WAS...
...DIFFERENT.
FIRST AID
OR, PERHAPS, SHE WAS THE ONE WHO WAS DIFFERENT.

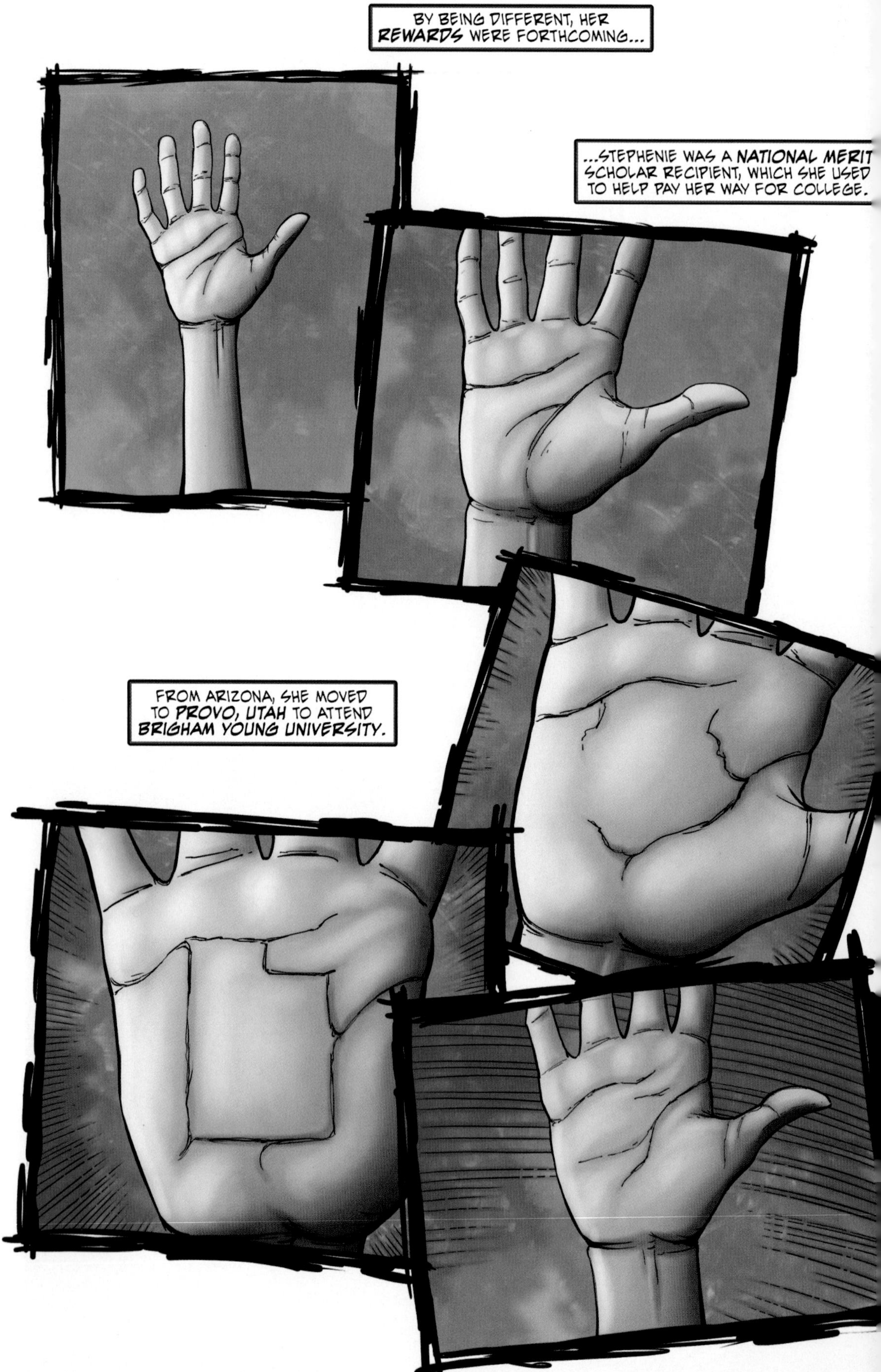

BY BEING DIFFERENT, HER REWARDS WERE FORTHCOMING...
...STEPHENIE WAS A NATIONAL MERIT SCHOLAR RECIPIENT, WHICH SHE USED TO HELP PAY HER WAY FOR COLLEGE.
FROM ARIZONA, SHE MOVED TO PROVO, UTAH TO ATTEND BRIGHAM YOUNG UNIVERSITY.

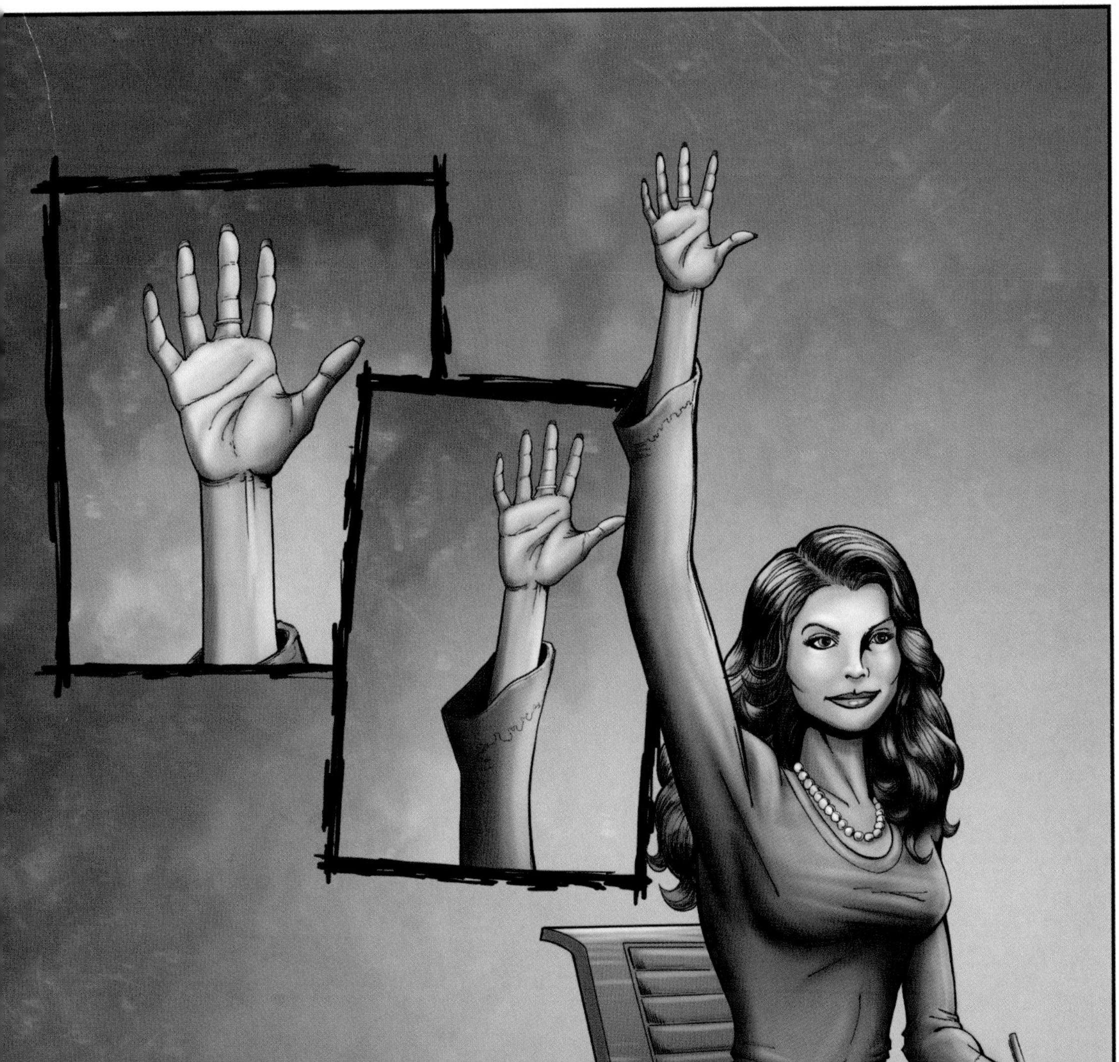

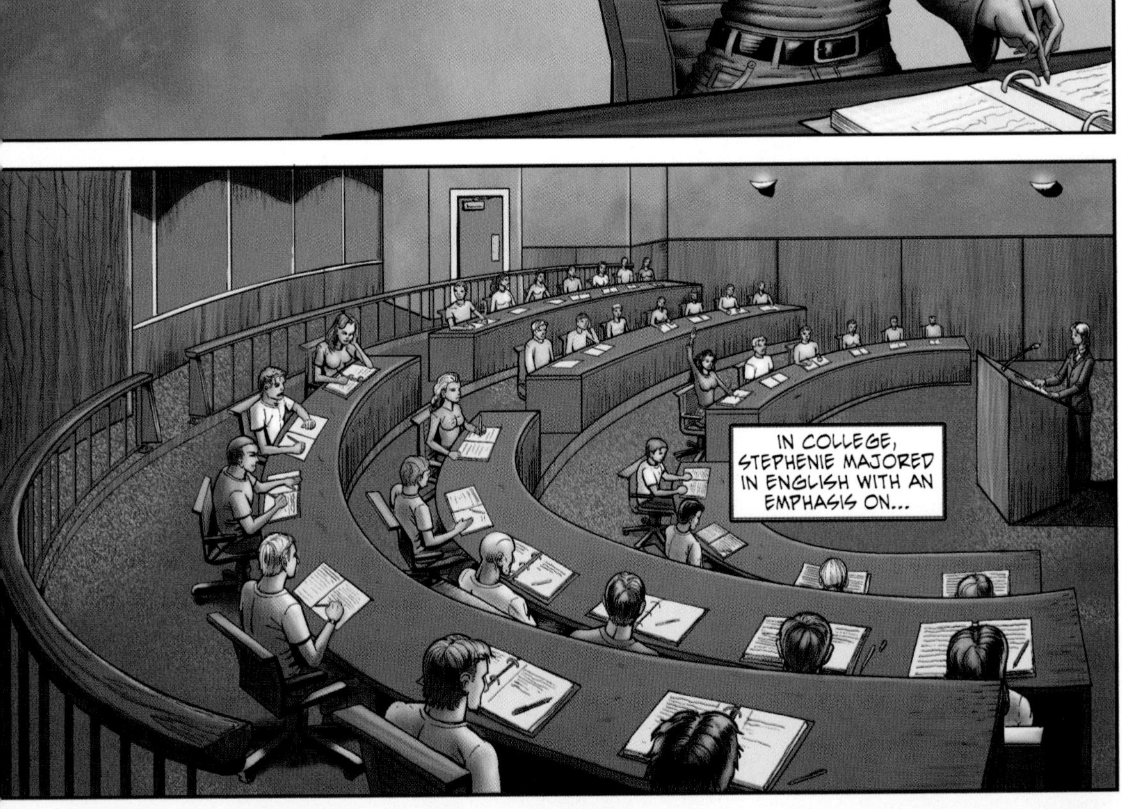
IN COLLEGE, STEPHENIE MAJORED IN ENGLISH WITH AN EMPHASIS ON...

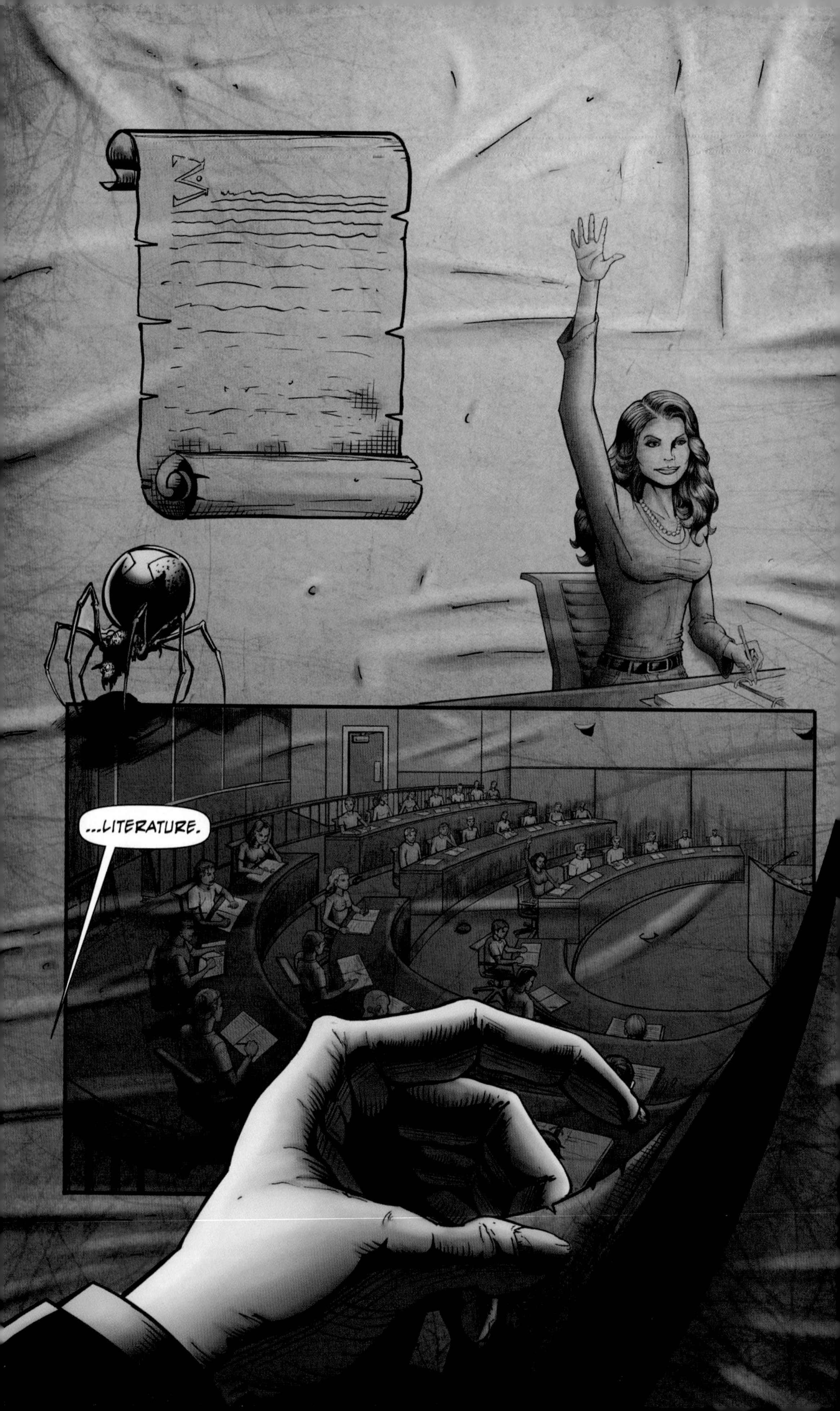
...LITERATURE.

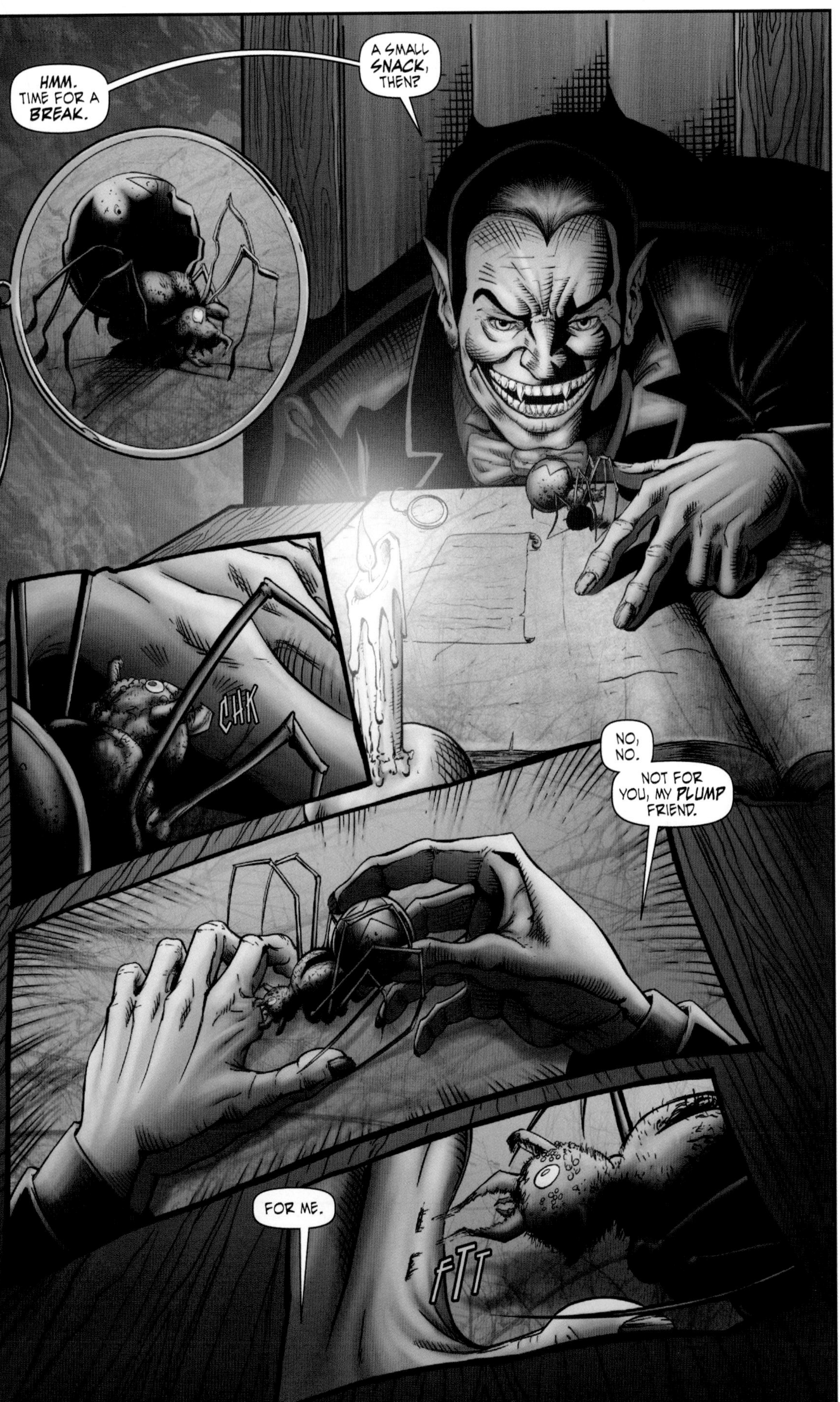
HMM. TIME FOR A BREAK.
A SMALL SNACK, THEN?
CHK
NO, NO.
NOT FOR YOU, MY PLUMP FRIEND.
FOR ME.
FTT

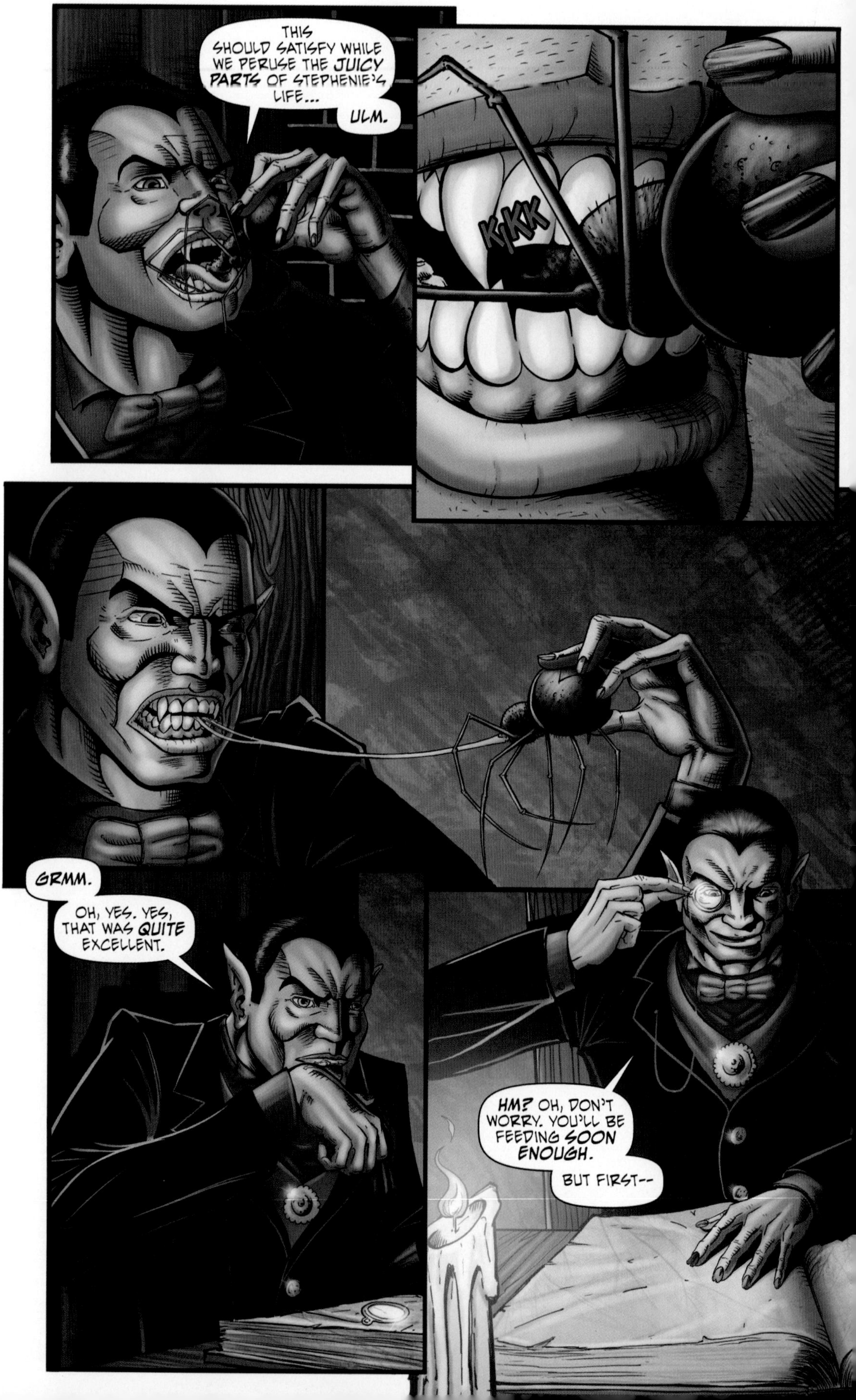
THIS SHOULD SATISFY WHILE WE PERUSE THE JUICY PARTS OF STEPHENIE'S LIFE...
ULM.
KIKK
GRMM.
OH, YES. YES, THAT WAS QUITE EXCELLENT.
HM? OH, DON'T WORRY. YOU'LL BE FEEDING SOON ENOUGH.
BUT FIRST--

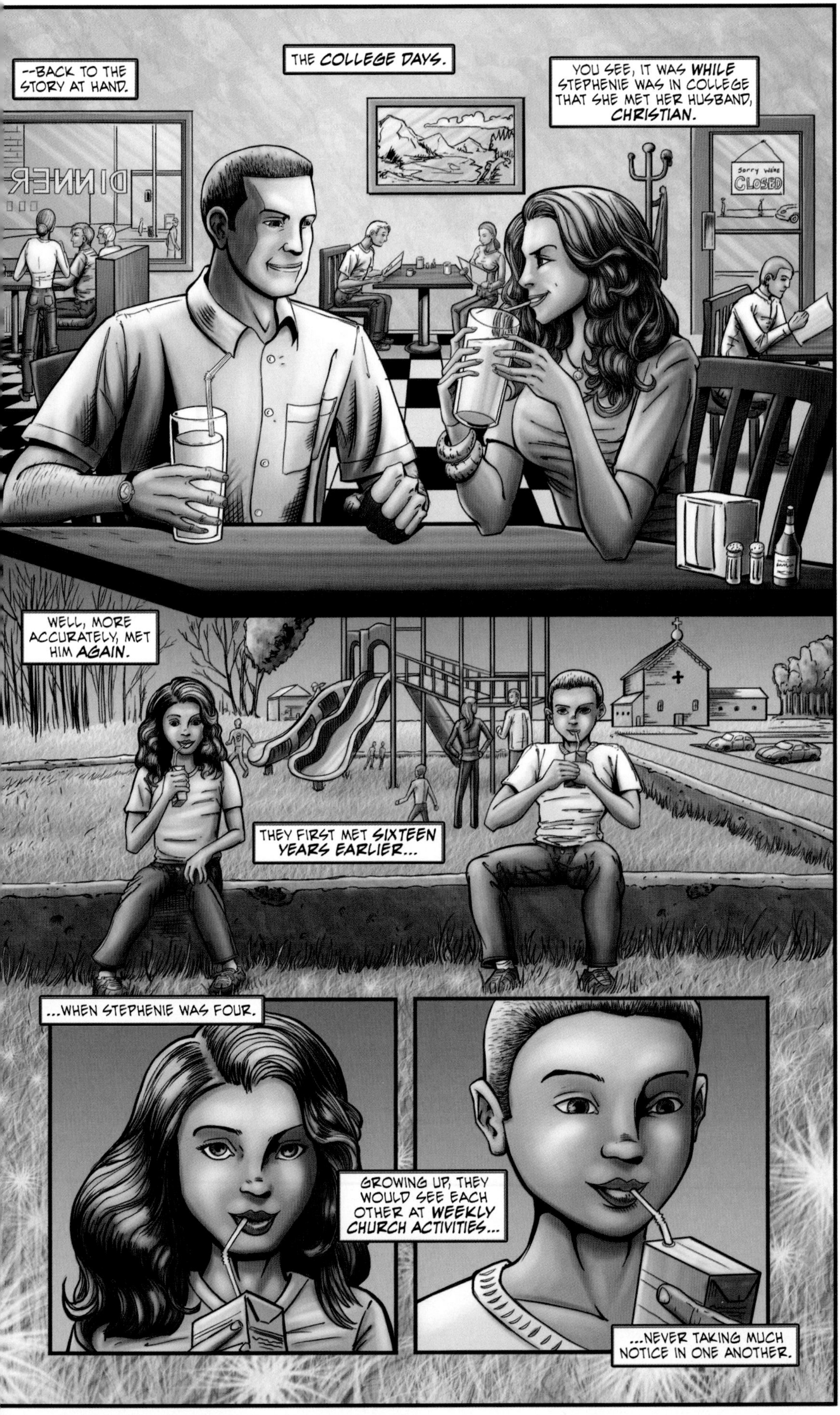
--BACK TO THE STORY AT HAND.
THE COLLEGE DAYS.
YOU SEE, IT WAS WHILE STEPHENIE WAS IN COLLEGE THAT SHE MET HER HUSBAND, CHRISTIAN.
DINNER
Sorry We're CLOSED
WELL, MORE ACCURATELY, MET HIM AGAIN.
THEY FIRST MET SIXTEEN YEARS EARLIER...
...WHEN STEPHENIE WAS FOUR.
GROWING UP, THEY WOULD SEE EACH OTHER AT WEEKLY CHURCH ACTIVITIES...
...NEVER TAKING MUCH NOTICE IN ONE ANOTHER.

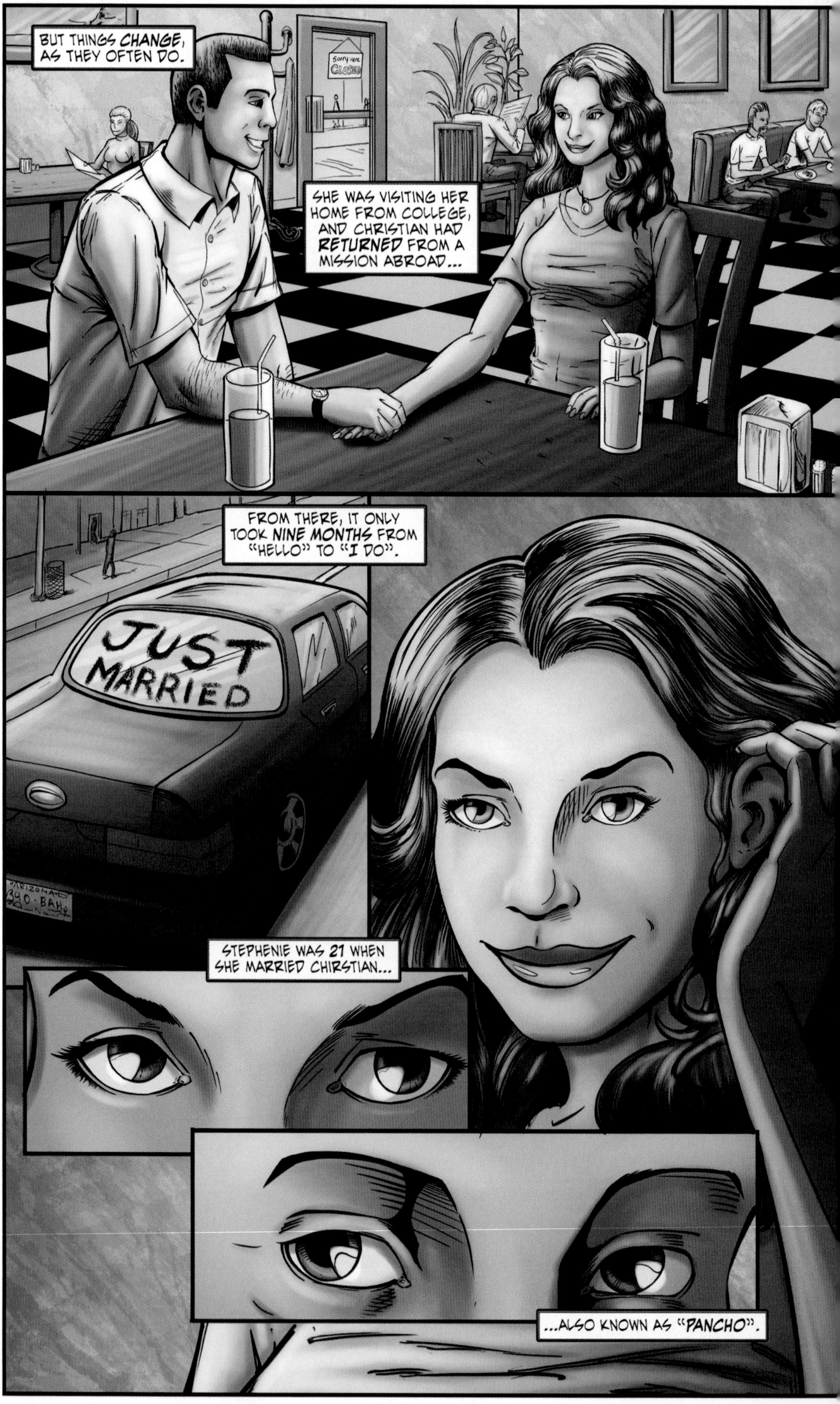
BUT THINGS CHANGE, AS THEY OFTEN DO.
SHE WAS VISITING HER HOME FROM COLLEGE, AND CHRISTIAN HAD RETURNED FROM A MISSION ABROAD...
FROM THERE, IT ONLY TOOK NINE MONTHS FROM "HELLO" TO "I DO".
JUST MARRIED
STEPHENIE WAS 21 WHEN SHE MARRIED CHIRSTIAN...
...ALSO KNOWN AS "PANCHO".

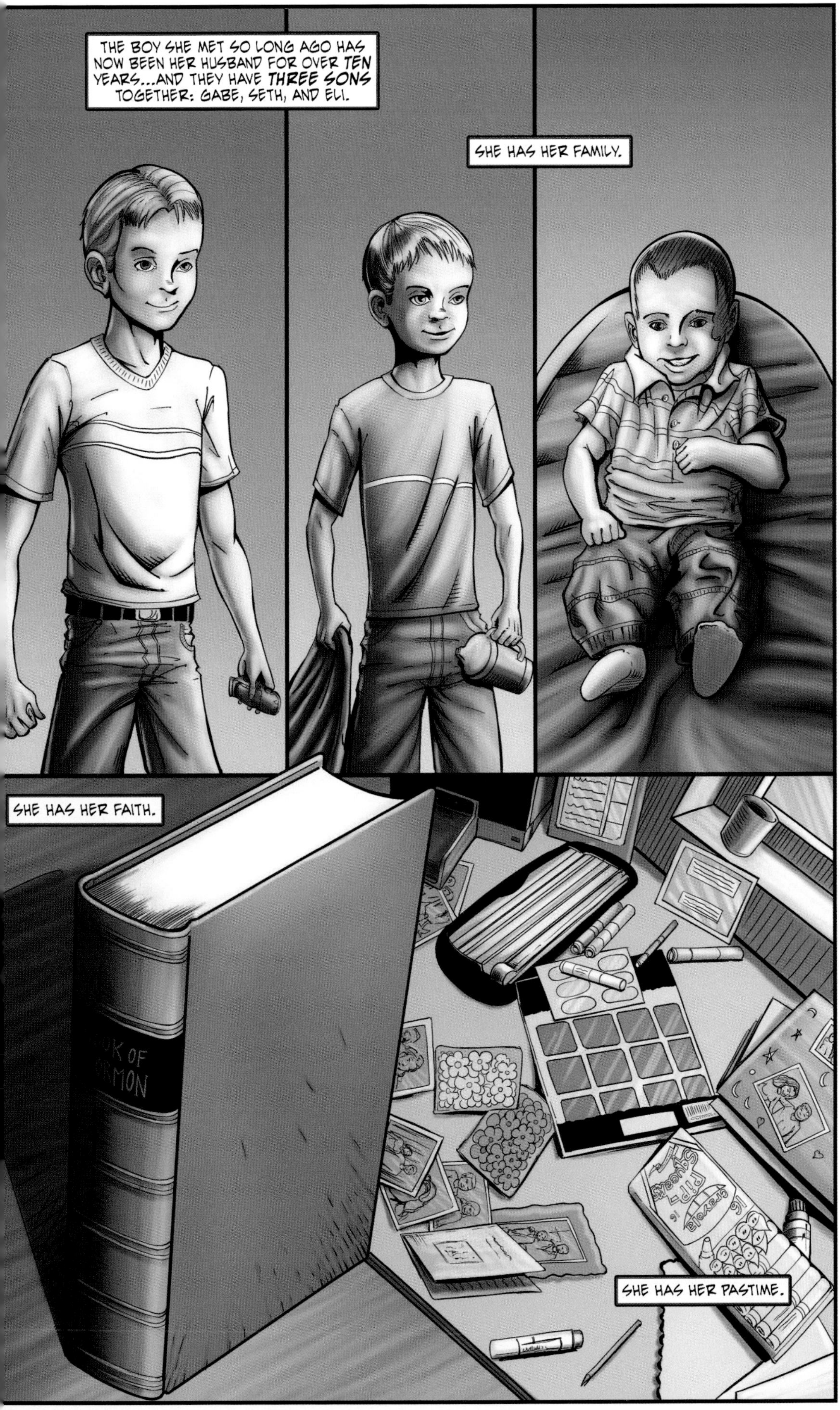
THE BOY SHE MET SO LONG AGO HAS NOW BEEN HER HUSBAND FOR OVER TEN YEARS...AND THEY HAVE THREE SONS TOGETHER: GABE, SETH, AND ELI.
SHE HAS HER FAMILY.
SHE HAS HER FAITH.
OK OF
RMON
SHE HAS HER PASTIME.

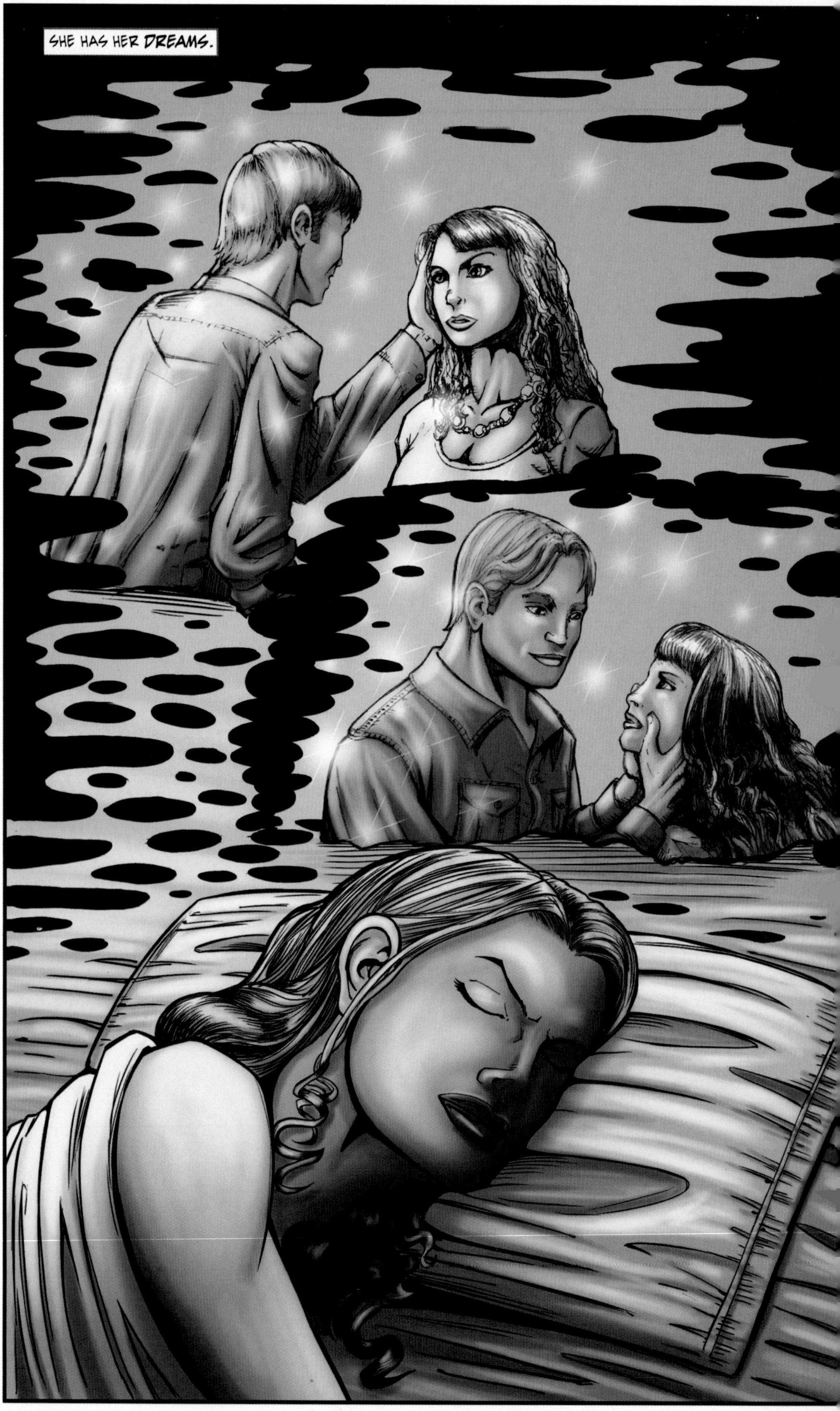
SHE HAS HER DREAMS.

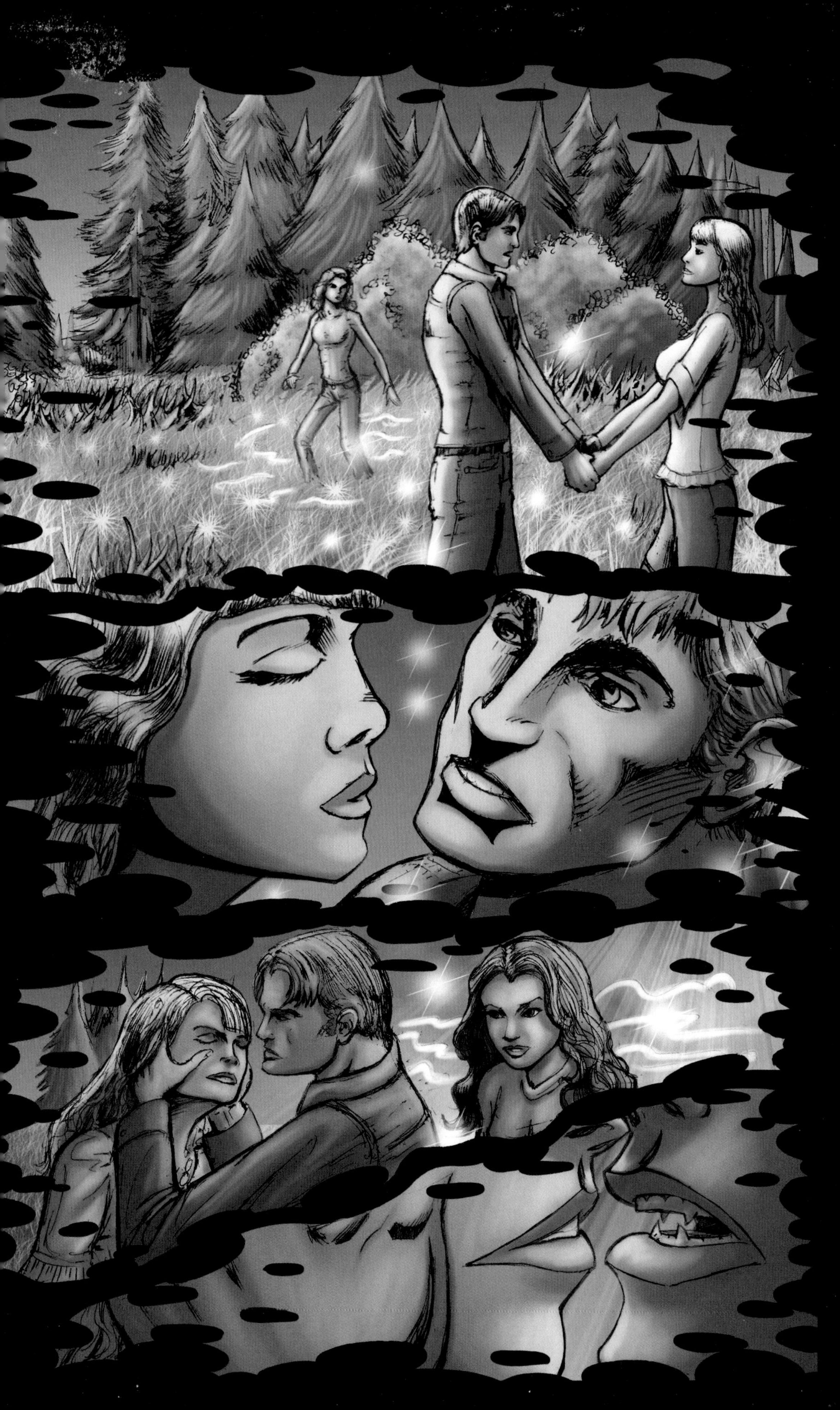

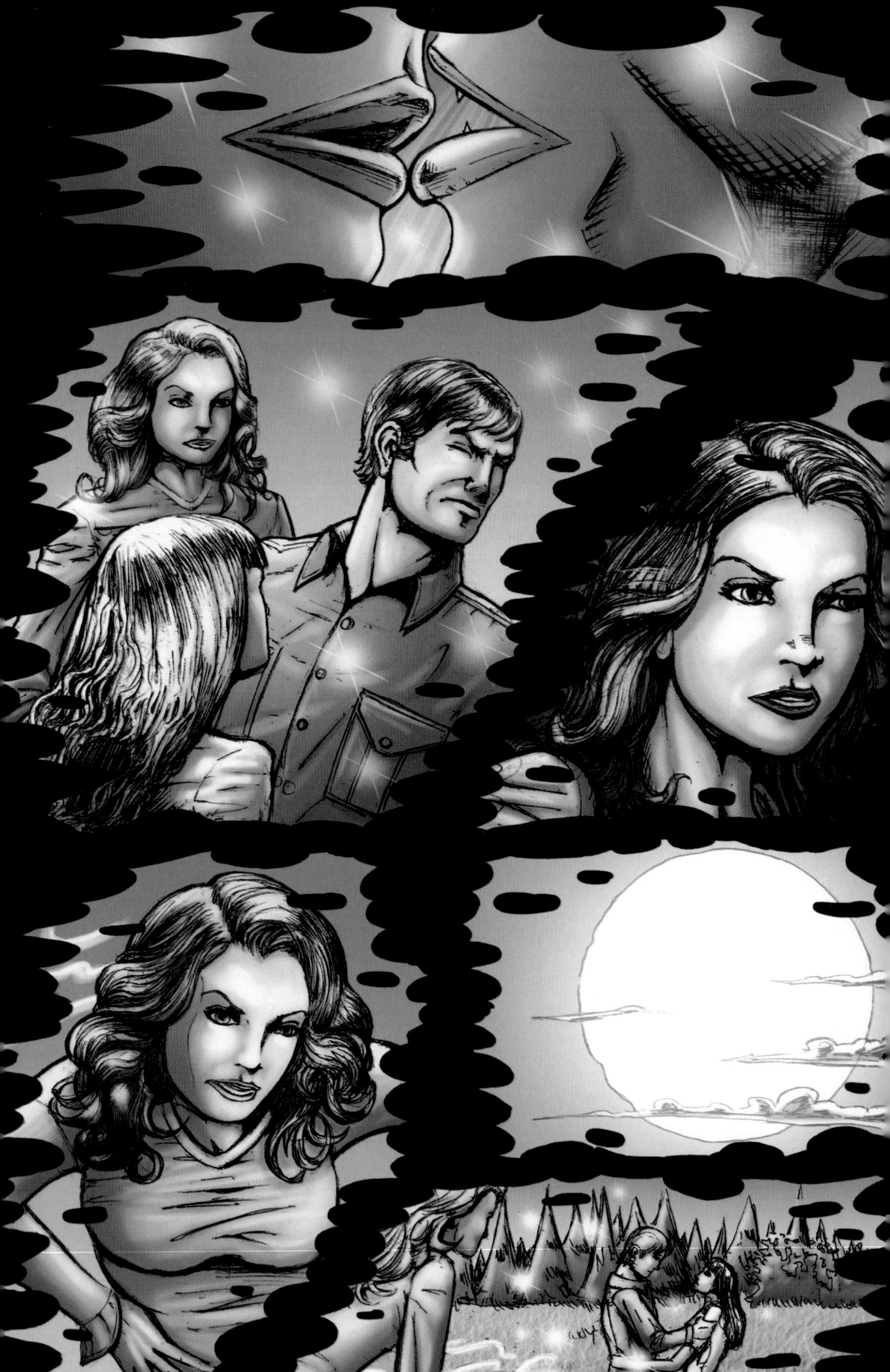

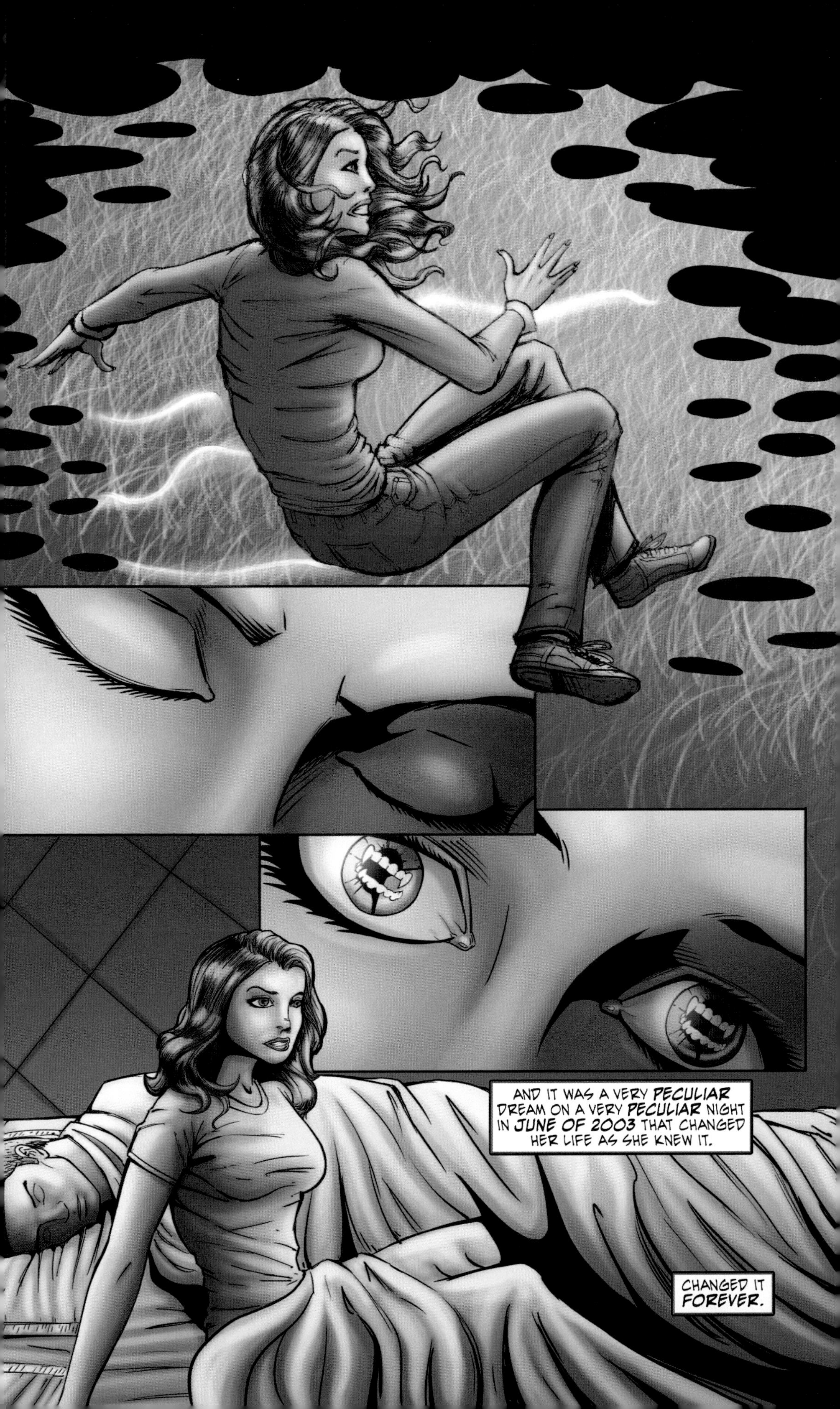
AND IT WAS A VERY PECULIAR DREAM ON A VERY PECULIAR NIGHT IN JUNE OF 2003 THAT CHANGED HER LIFE AS SHE KNEW IT.
CHANGED IT FOREVER.

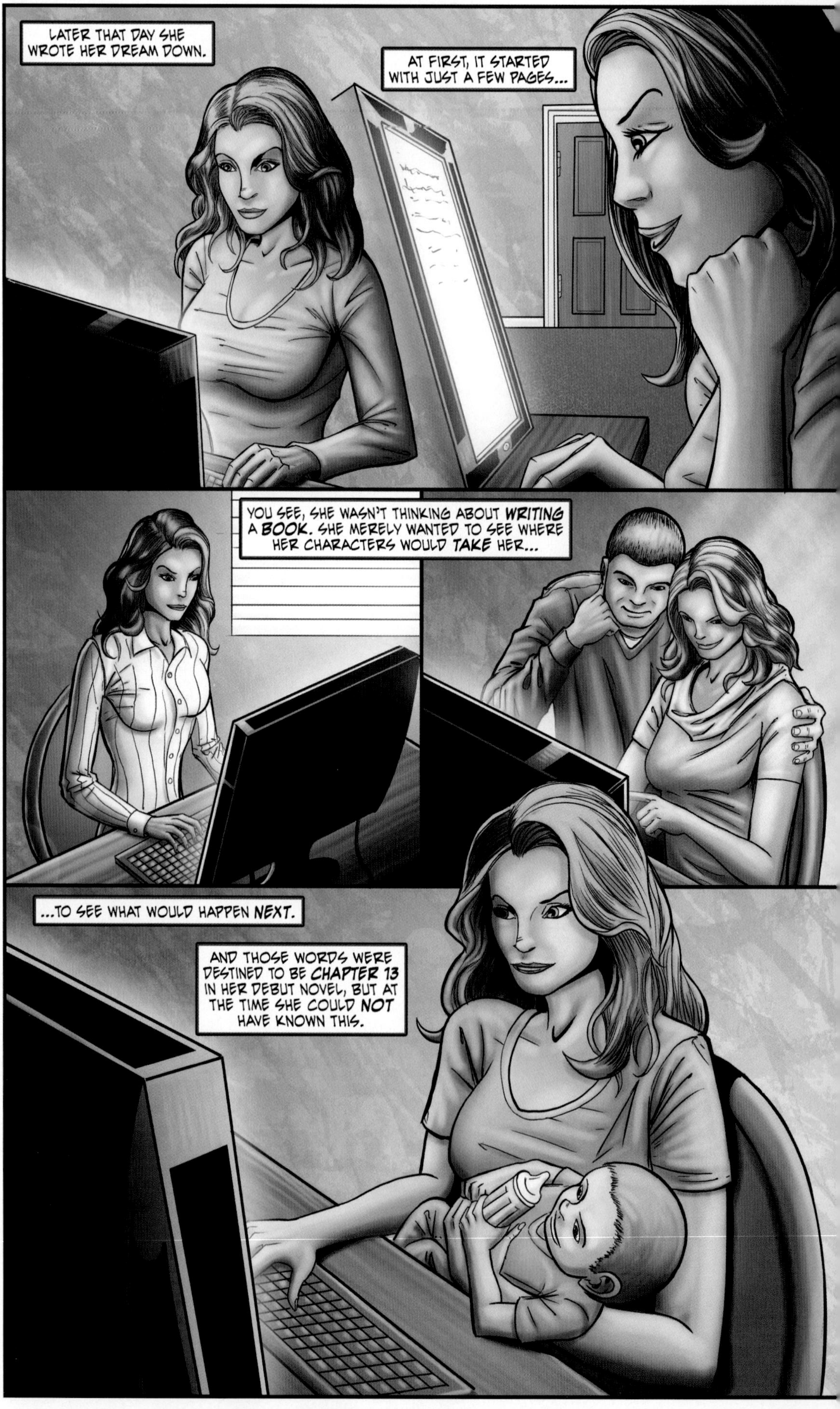
LATER THAT DAY SHE WROTE HER DREAM DOWN.
AT FIRST, IT STARTED WITH JUST A FEW PAGES...
YOU SEE, SHE WASN'T THINKING ABOUT WRITING A BOOK. SHE MERELY WANTED TO SEE WHERE HER CHARACTERS WOULD TAKE HER...
...TO SEE WHAT WOULD HAPPEN NEXT.
AND THOSE WORDS WERE DESTINED TO BE CHAPTER 13 IN HER DEBUT NOVEL, BUT AT THE TIME SHE COULD NOT HAVE KNOWN THIS.

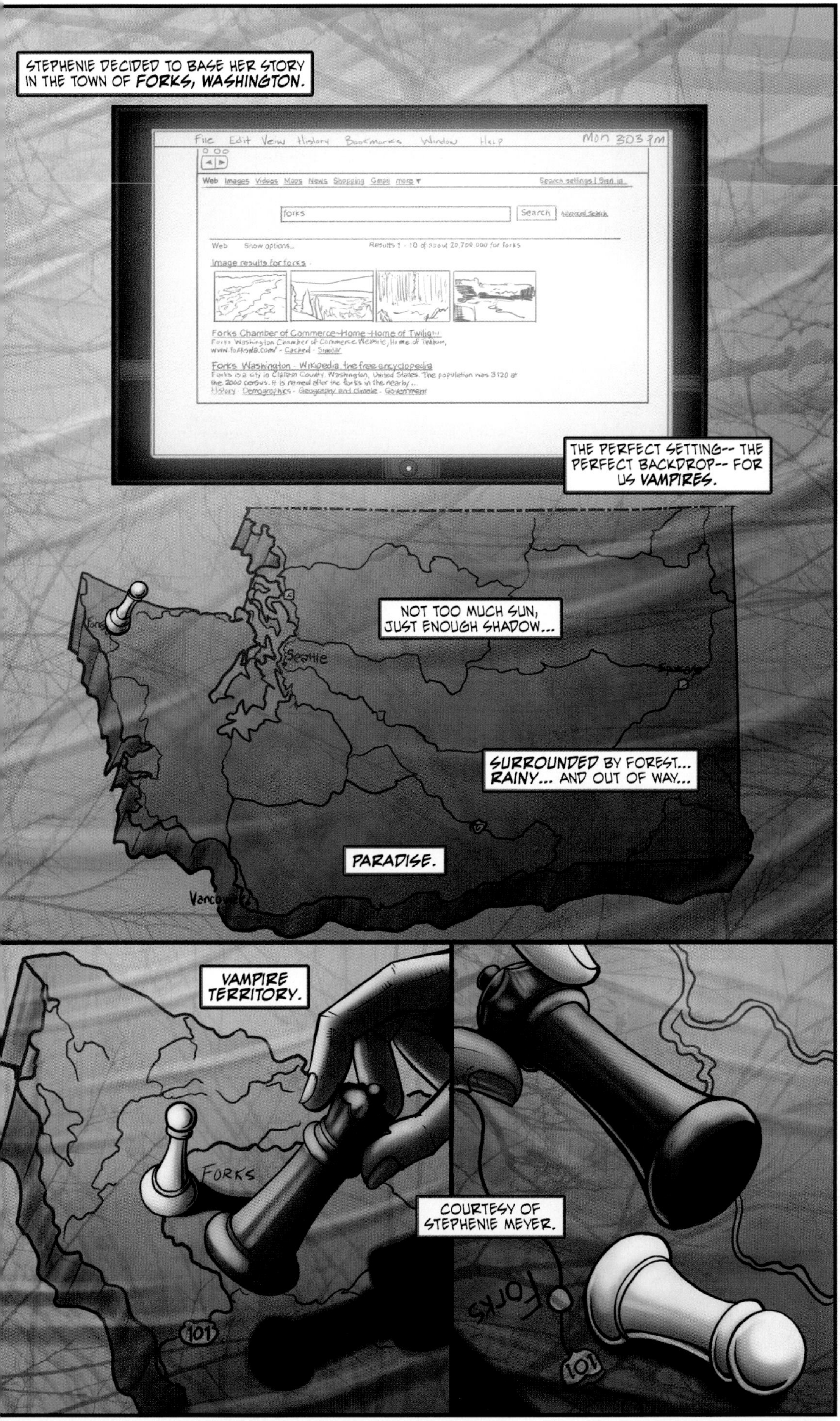
STEPHENIE DECIDED TO BASE HER STORY IN THE TOWN OF FORKS, WASHINGTON.
forks
Search
THE PERFECT SETTING-- THE PERFECT BACKDROP-- FOR US VAMPIRES.
NOT TOO MUCH SUN, JUST ENOUGH SHADOW...
Seattle
SURROUNDED BY FOREST... RAINY... AND OUT OF WAY...
PARADISE.
VAMPIRE TERRITORY.
FORKS
101
COURTESY OF STEPHENIE MEYER.

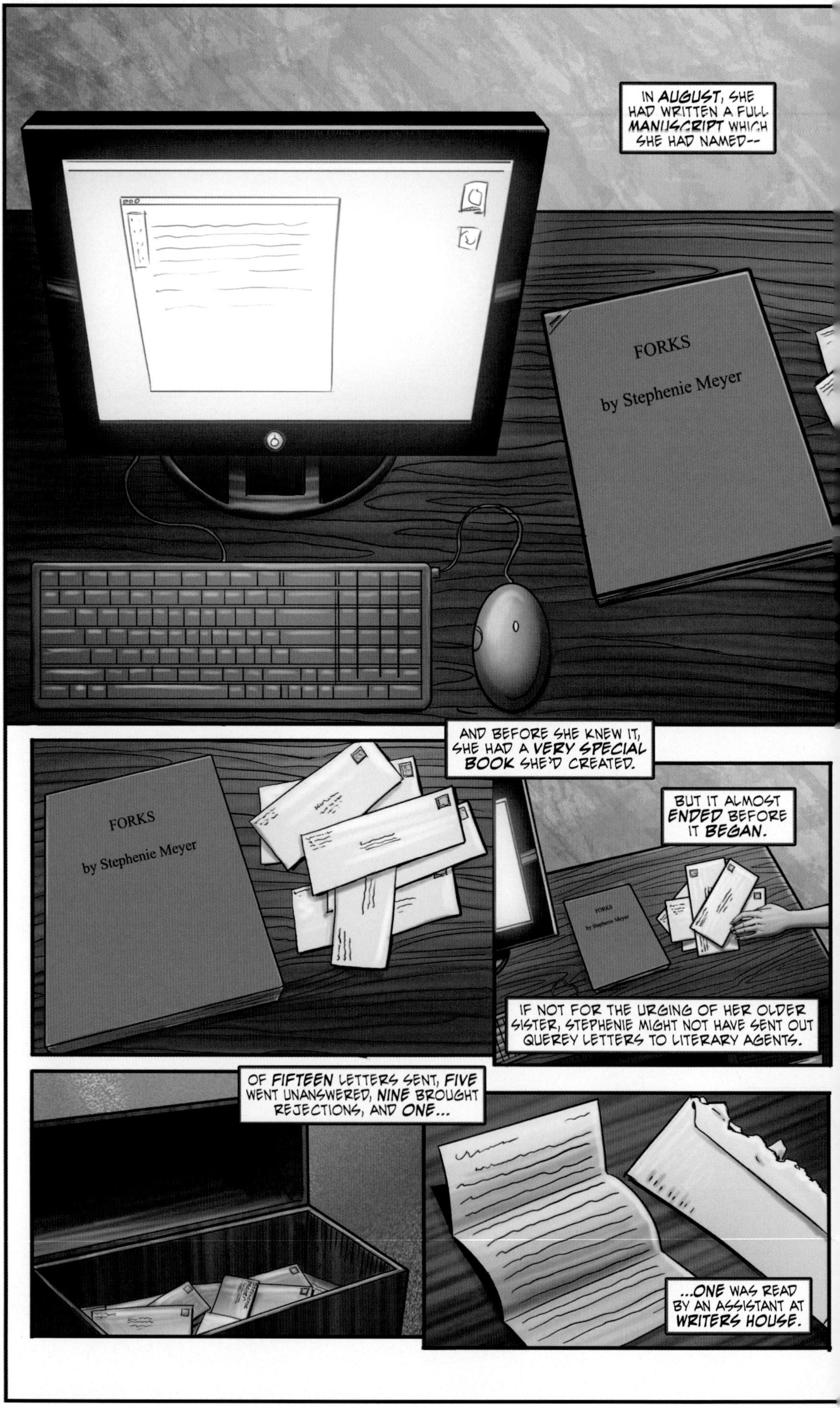
IN AUGUST, SHE HAD WRITTEN A FULL MANUSCRIPT WHICH SHE HAD NAMED--
FORKS
by Stephenie Meyer
AND BEFORE SHE KNEW IT, SHE HAD A VERY SPECIAL BOOK SHE'D CREATED.
FORKS
by Stephenie Meyer
BUT IT ALMOST ENDED BEFORE IT BEGAN.
FORKS
by Stephenie Meyer
IF NOT FOR THE URGING OF HER OLDER SISTER, STEPHENIE MIGHT NOT HAVE SENT OUT QUEREY LETTERS TO LITERARY AGENTS.
OF FIFTEEN LETTERS SENT, FIVE WENT UNANSWERED, NINE BROUGHT REJECTIONS, AND ONE...
...ONE WAS READ BY AN ASSISTANT AT WRITERS HOUSE.

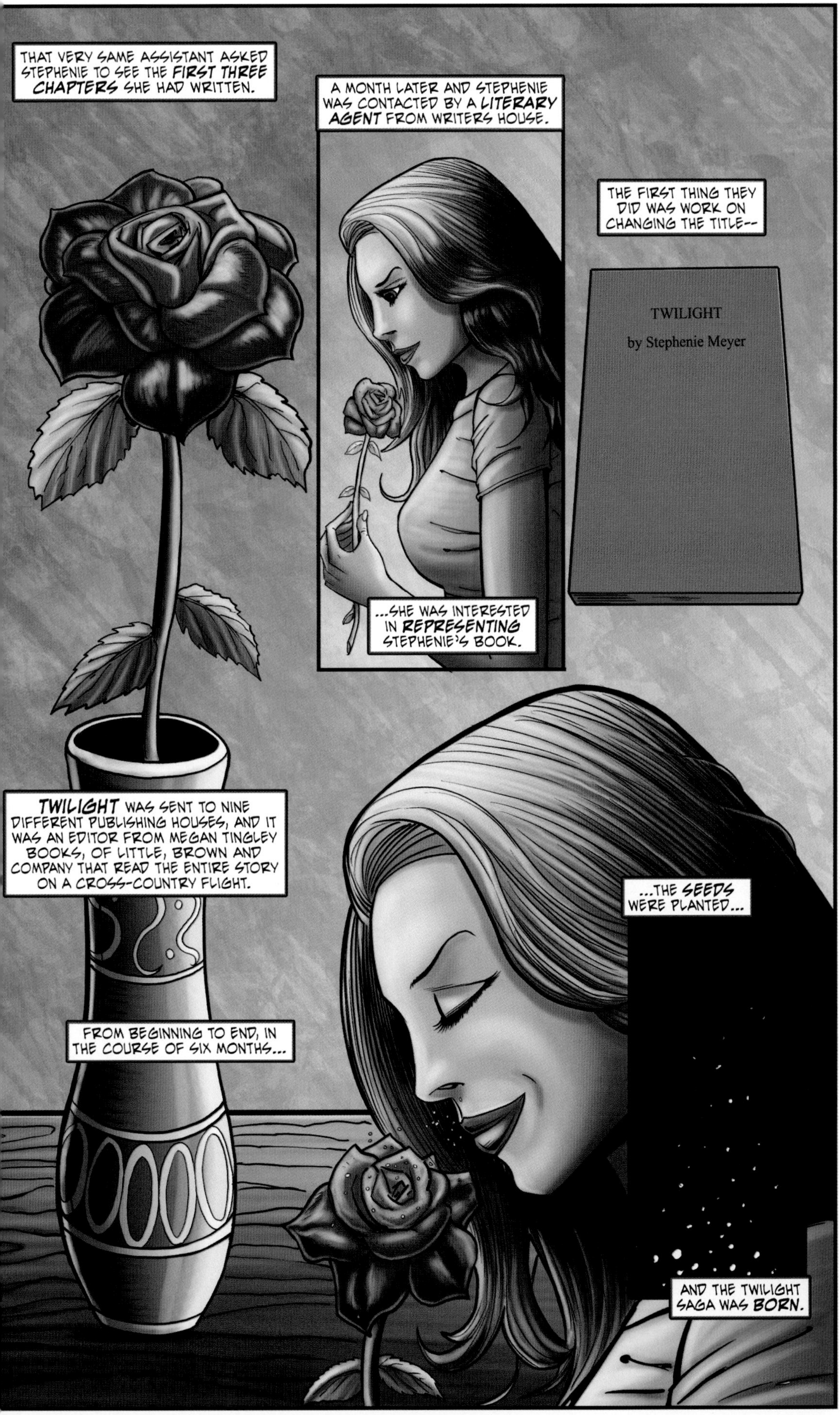
THAT VERY SAME ASSISTANT ASKED STEPHENIE TO SEE THE FIRST THREE CHAPTERS SHE HAD WRITTEN.
A MONTH LATER AND STEPHENIE WAS CONTACTED BY A LITERARY AGENT FROM WRITERS HOUSE.
...SHE WAS INTERESTED IN REPRESENTING STEPHENIE'S BOOK.
THE FIRST THING THEY DID WAS WORK ON CHANGING THE TITLE--
TWILIGHT
by Stephenie Meyer
TWILIGHT WAS SENT TO NINE DIFFERENT PUBLISHING HOUSES, AND IT WAS AN EDITOR FROM MEGAN TINGLEY BOOKS, OF LITTLE, BROWN AND COMPANY THAT READ THE ENTIRE STORY ON A CROSS-COUNTRY FLIGHT.
FROM BEGINNING TO END, IN THE COURSE OF SIX MONTHS...
...THE SEEDS WERE PLANTED...
AND THE TWILIGHT SAGA WAS BORN.

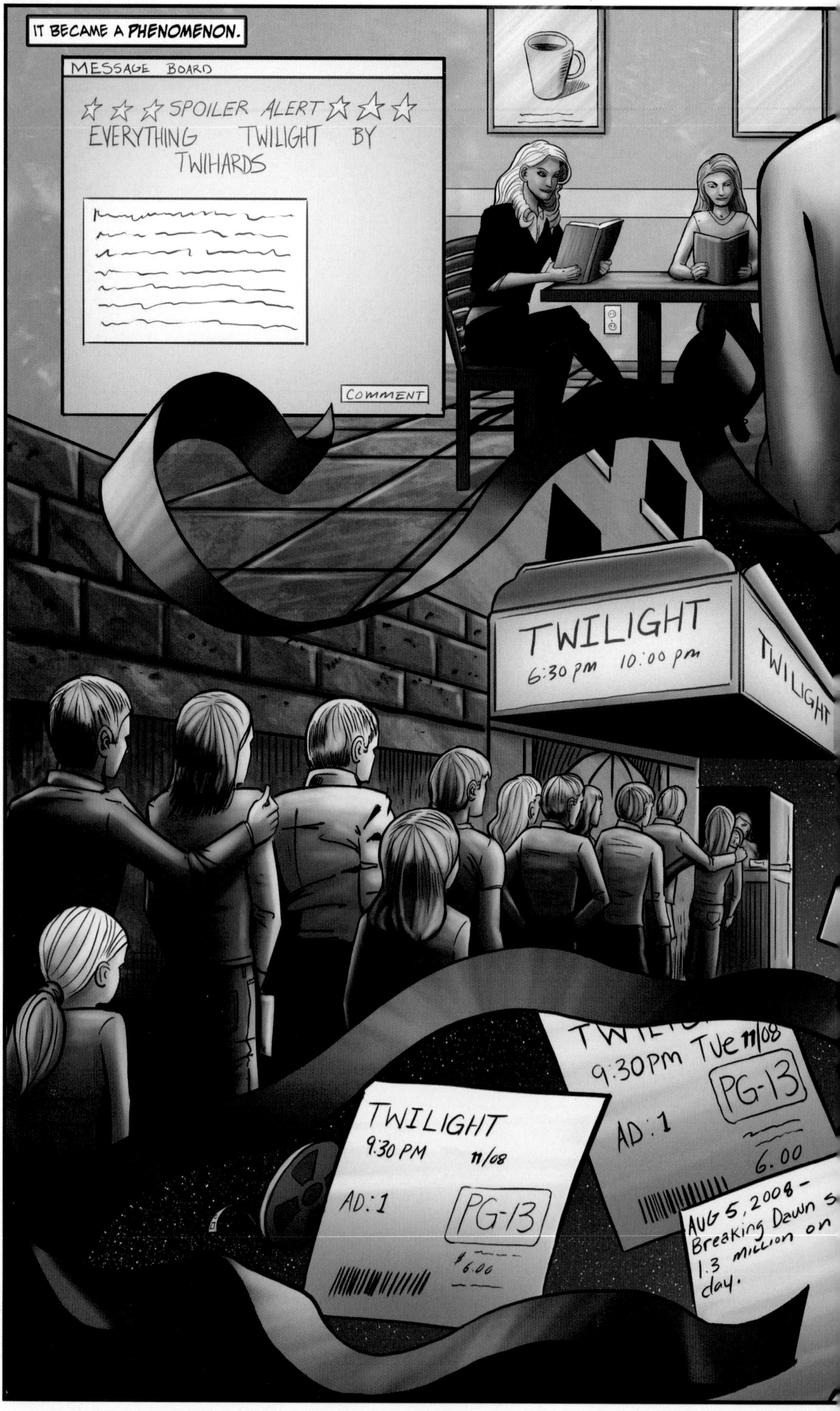
IT BECAME A PHENOMENON.
MESSAGE BOARD
☆☆☆SPOILER ALERT☆☆☆
EVERYTHING TWILIGHT BY TWIHARDS
COMMENT
TWILIGHT
6:30 pm 10:00 pm
TWILIGHT
9:30PM Tue 11/08
PG-13
AD:1
6.00
TWILIGHT
9:30 PM 11/08
AD:1
PG-13
$6.00
AUG 5, 2008 –
Breaking Dawn
1.3 million on
day.

and so the Lion fell
TEAM EDWARD
TEAM JACOB
Dazzled by Twilight
Twilight

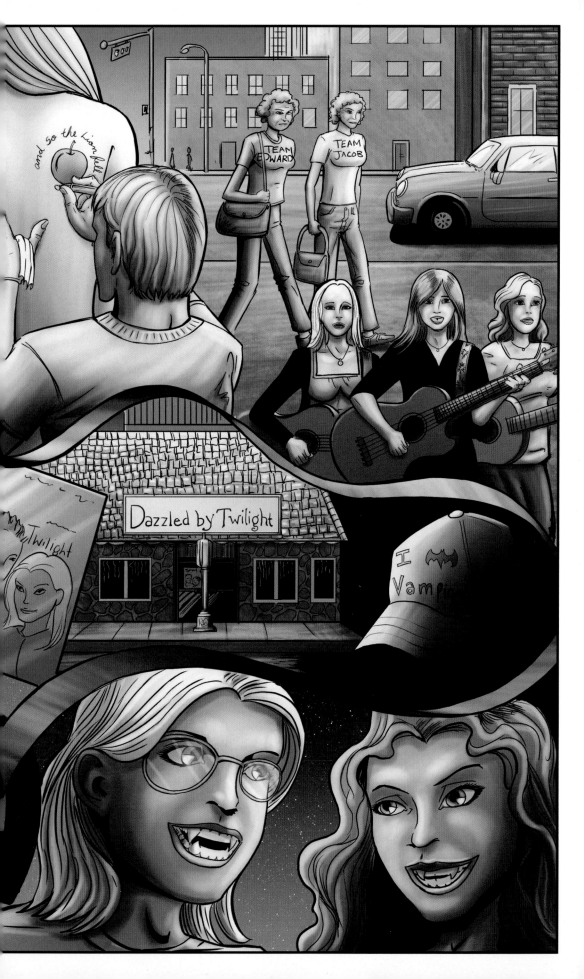

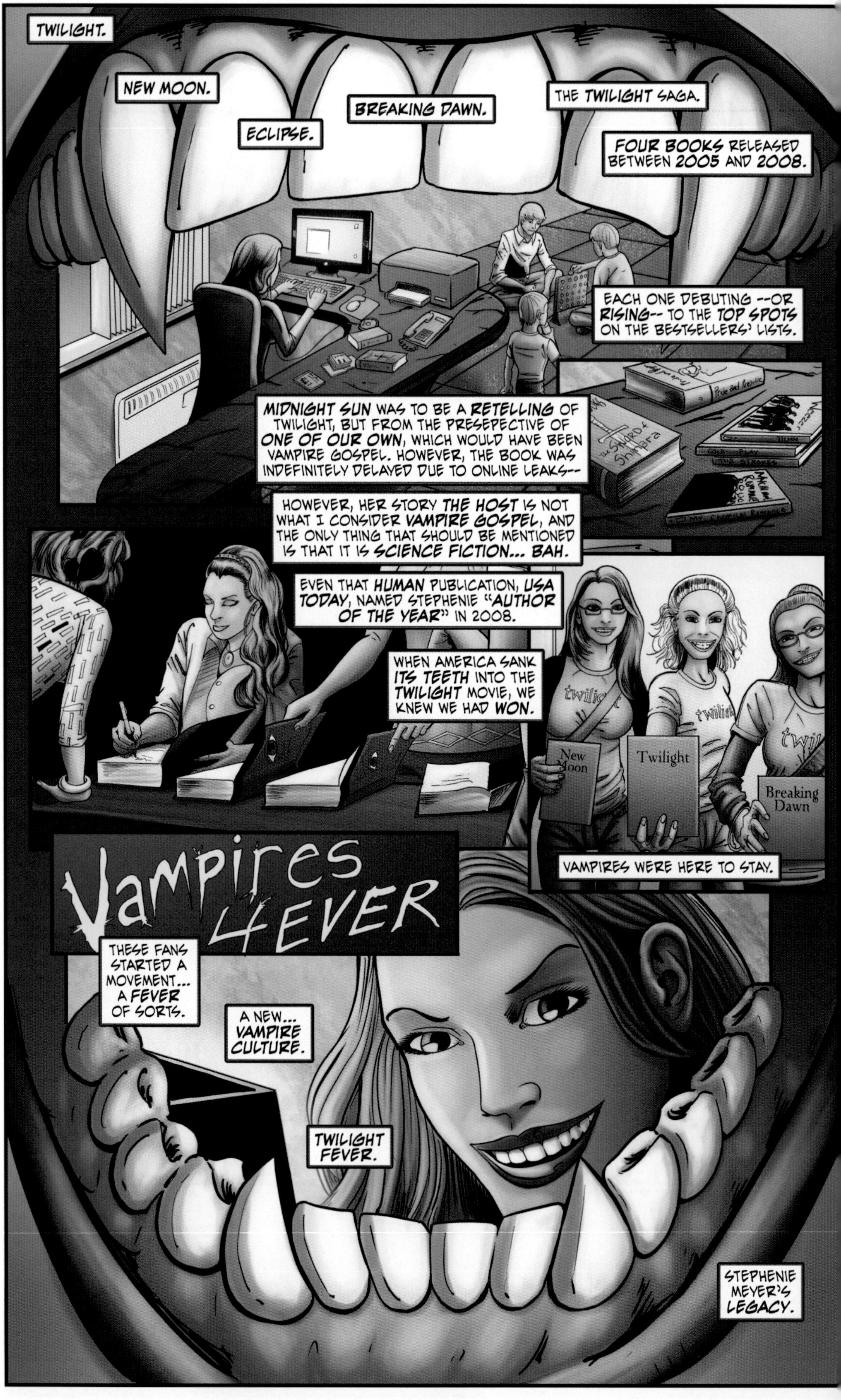

TWILIGHT.
NEW MOON.
ECLIPSE.
BREAKING DAWN.
THE TWILIGHT SAGA.
FOUR BOOKS RELEASED BETWEEN 2005 AND 2008.
EACH ONE DEBUTING --OR RISING-- TO THE TOP SPOTS ON THE BESTSELLERS' LISTS.
MIDNIGHT SUN WAS TO BE A RETELLING OF TWILIGHT, BUT FROM THE PRESEPECTIVE OF ONE OF OUR OWN, WHICH WOULD HAVE BEEN VAMPIRE GOSPEL. HOWEVER, THE BOOK WAS INDEFINITELY DELAYED DUE TO ONLINE LEAKS--
HOWEVER, HER STORY THE HOST IS NOT WHAT I CONSIDER VAMPIRE GOSPEL, AND THE ONLY THING THAT SHOULD BE MENTIONED IS THAT IT IS SCIENCE FICTION... BAH.
EVEN THAT HUMAN PUBLICATION, USA TODAY, NAMED STEPHENIE "AUTHOR OF THE YEAR" IN 2008.
WHEN AMERICA SANK ITS TEETH INTO THE TWILIGHT MOVIE, WE KNEW WE HAD WON.
New Moon
Twilight
Breaking Dawn
VAMPIRES WERE HERE TO STAY.
Vampires 4EVER
THESE FANS STARTED A MOVEMENT... A FEVER OF SORTS.
A NEW... VAMPIRE CULTURE.
TWILIGHT FEVER.
STEPHENIE MEYER'S LEGACY.

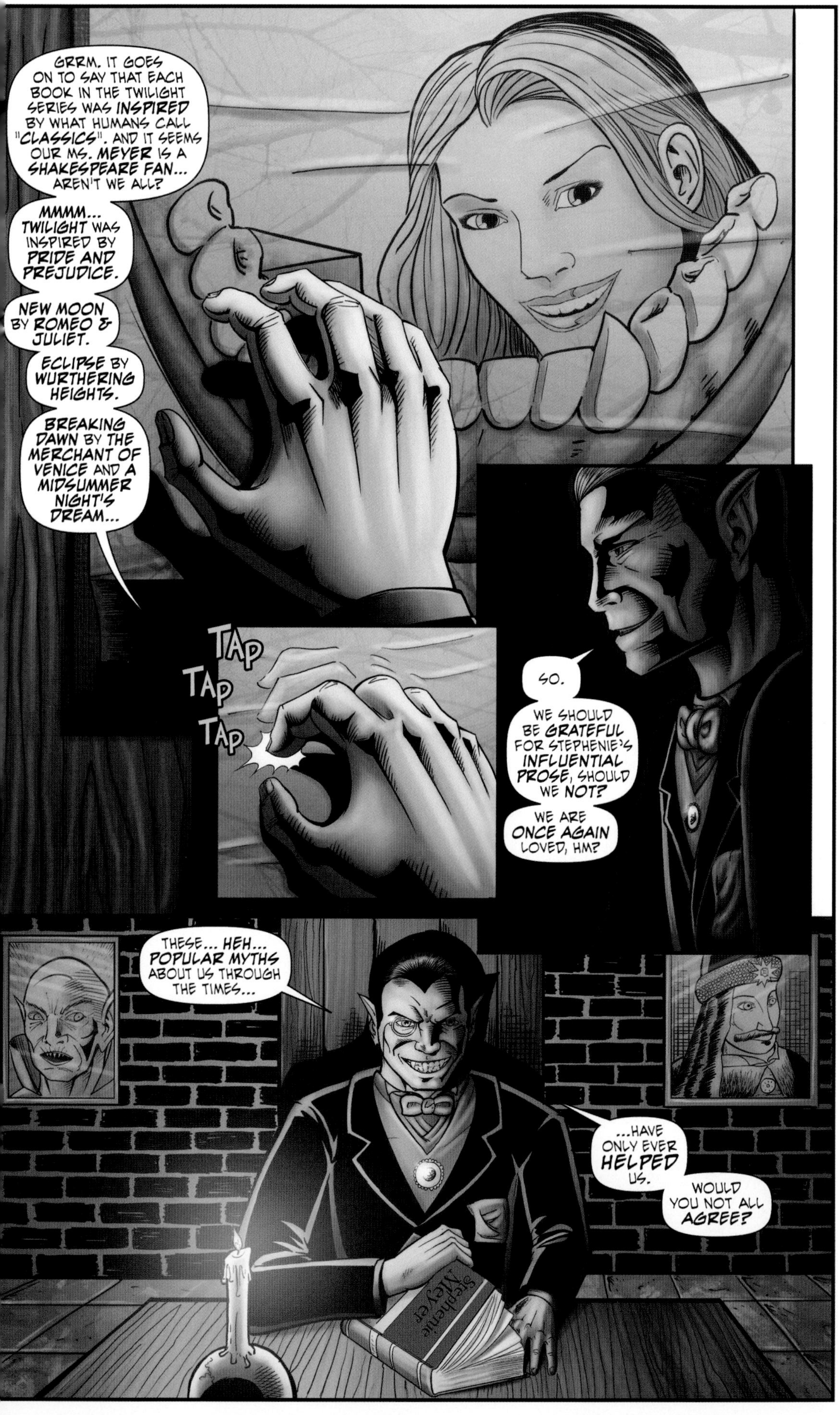
GRRM. IT GOES ON TO SAY THAT EACH BOOK IN THE TWILIGHT SERIES WAS INSPIRED BY WHAT HUMANS CALL "CLASSICS". AND IT SEEMS OUR MS. MEYER IS A SHAKESPEARE FAN... AREN'T WE ALL?
MMMM... TWILIGHT WAS INSPIRED BY PRIDE AND PREJUDICE.
NEW MOON BY ROMEO & JULIET.
ECLIPSE BY WURTHERING HEIGHTS.
BREAKING DAWN BY THE MERCHANT OF VENICE AND A MIDSUMMER NIGHT'S DREAM...
TAP
TAP
TAP
SO.
WE SHOULD BE GRATEFUL FOR STEPHENIE'S INFLUENTIAL PROSE, SHOULD WE NOT?
WE ARE ONCE AGAIN LOVED, HM?
THESE... HEH... POPULAR MYTHS ABOUT US THROUGH THE TIMES...
...HAVE ONLY EVER HELPED US.
WOULD YOU NOT ALL AGREE?
Stephenie Meyer

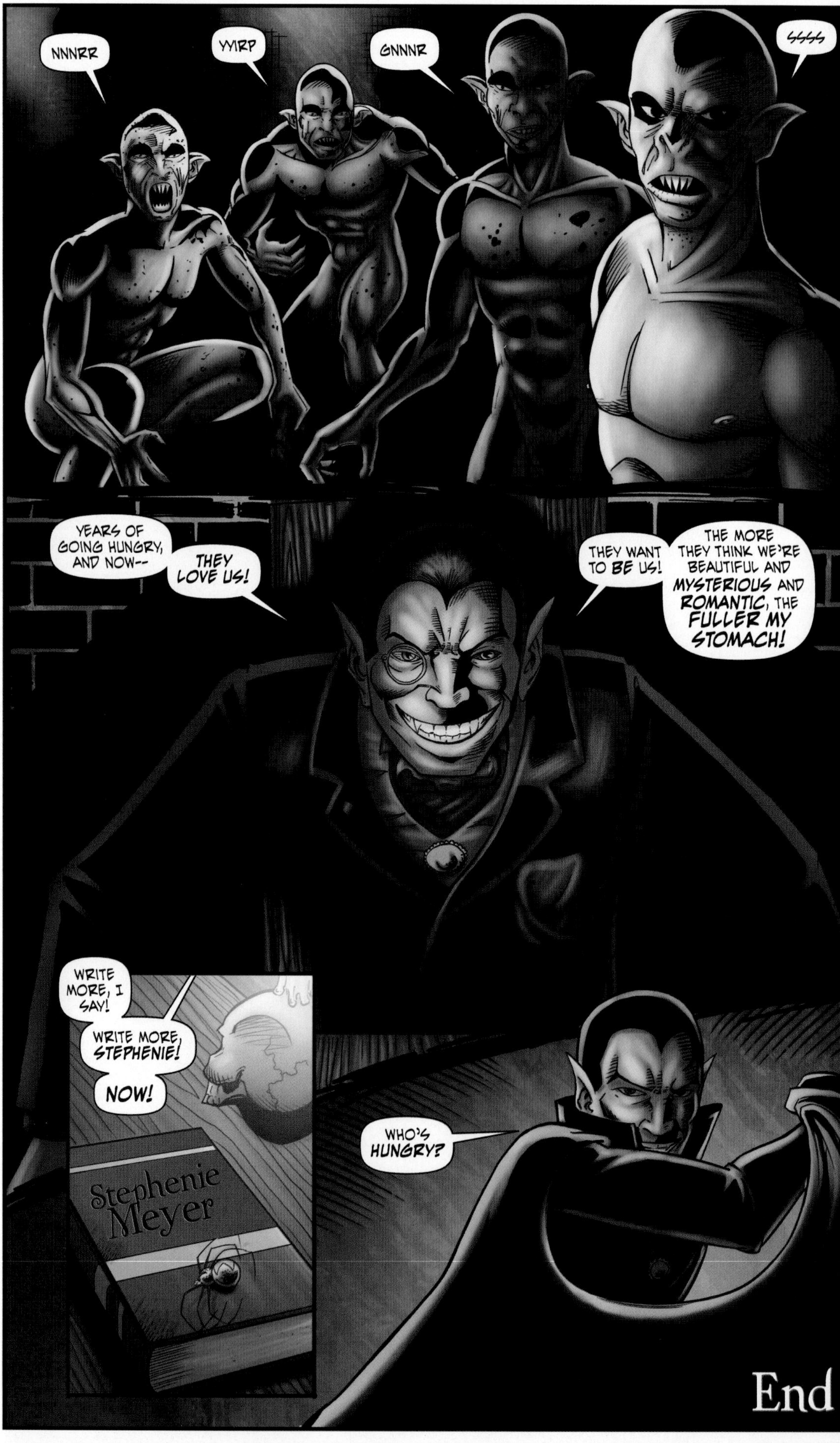
NNNRR
YYIRP
GNNNR
SSSS
YEARS OF GOING HUNGRY, AND NOW--
THEY LOVE US!
THEY WANT TO BE US!
THE MORE THEY THINK WE'RE BEAUTIFUL AND MYSTERIOUS AND ROMANTIC, THE FULLER MY STOMACH!
WRITE MORE, I SAY!
WRITE MORE, STEPHENIE!
NOW!
Stephenie Meyer
WHO'S HUNGRY?
End

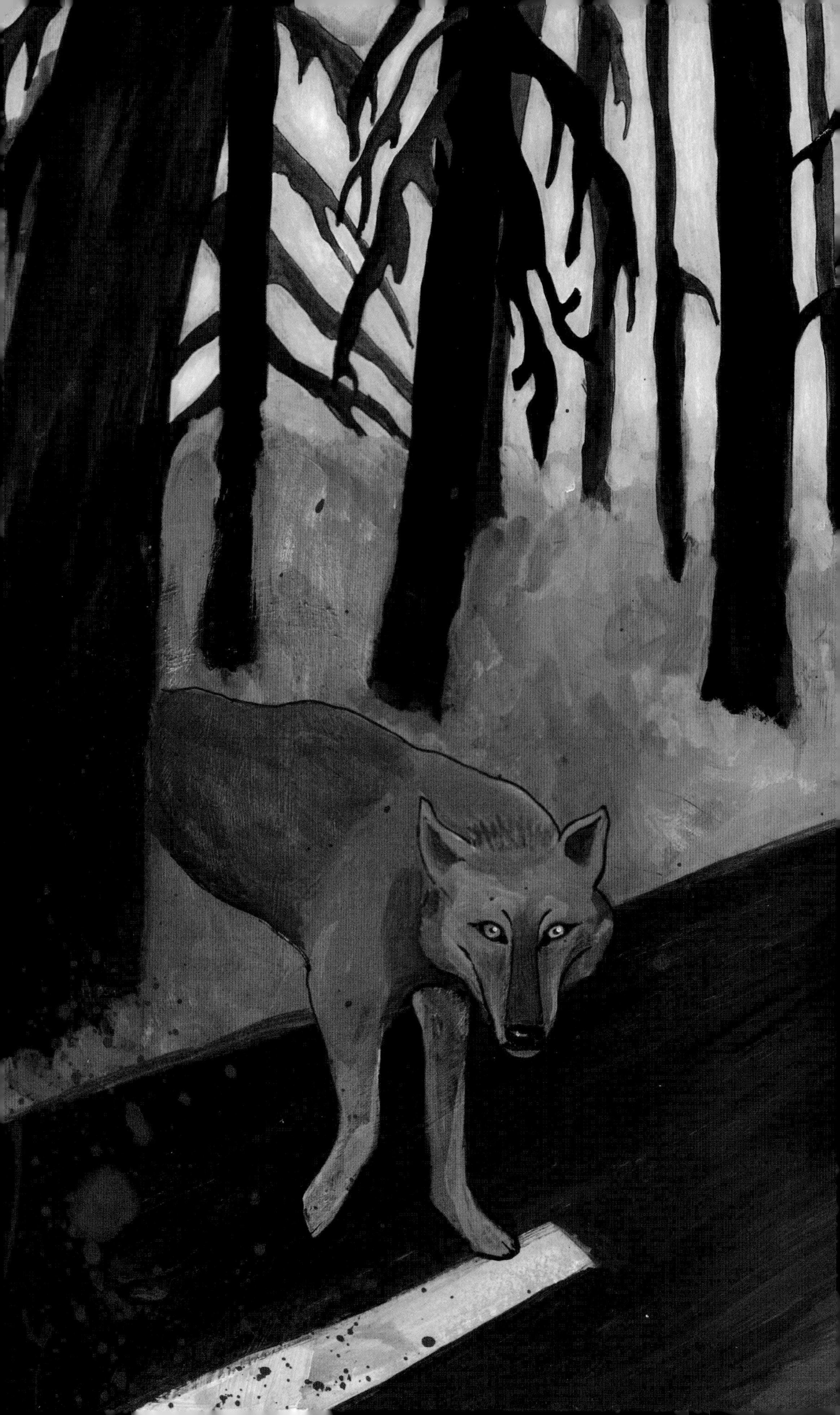

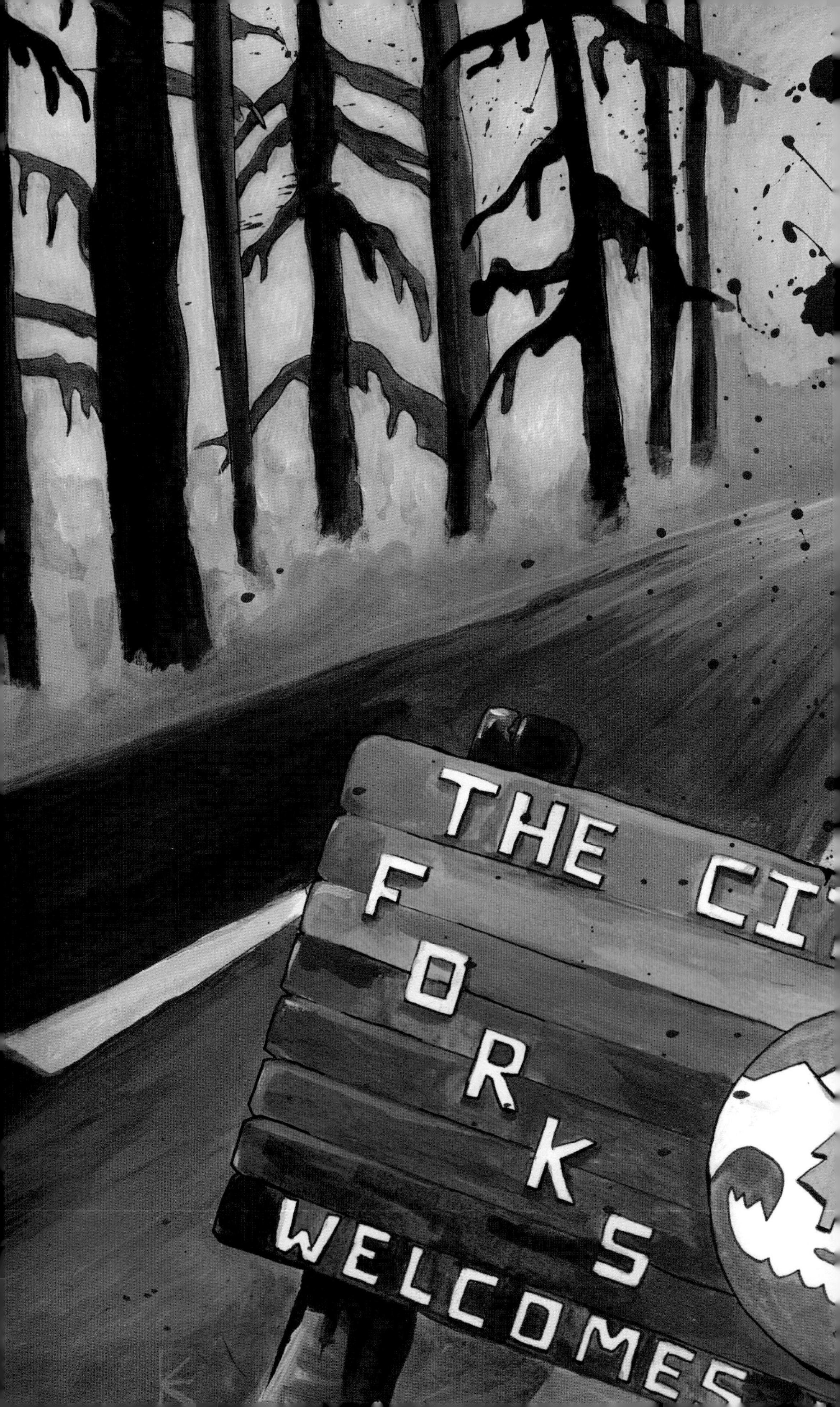
THE
FORKS
WELCOME

THE HISTORY OF FORKS

WORDS BY DARREN DAVIS
ART BY MATT BELLISLE

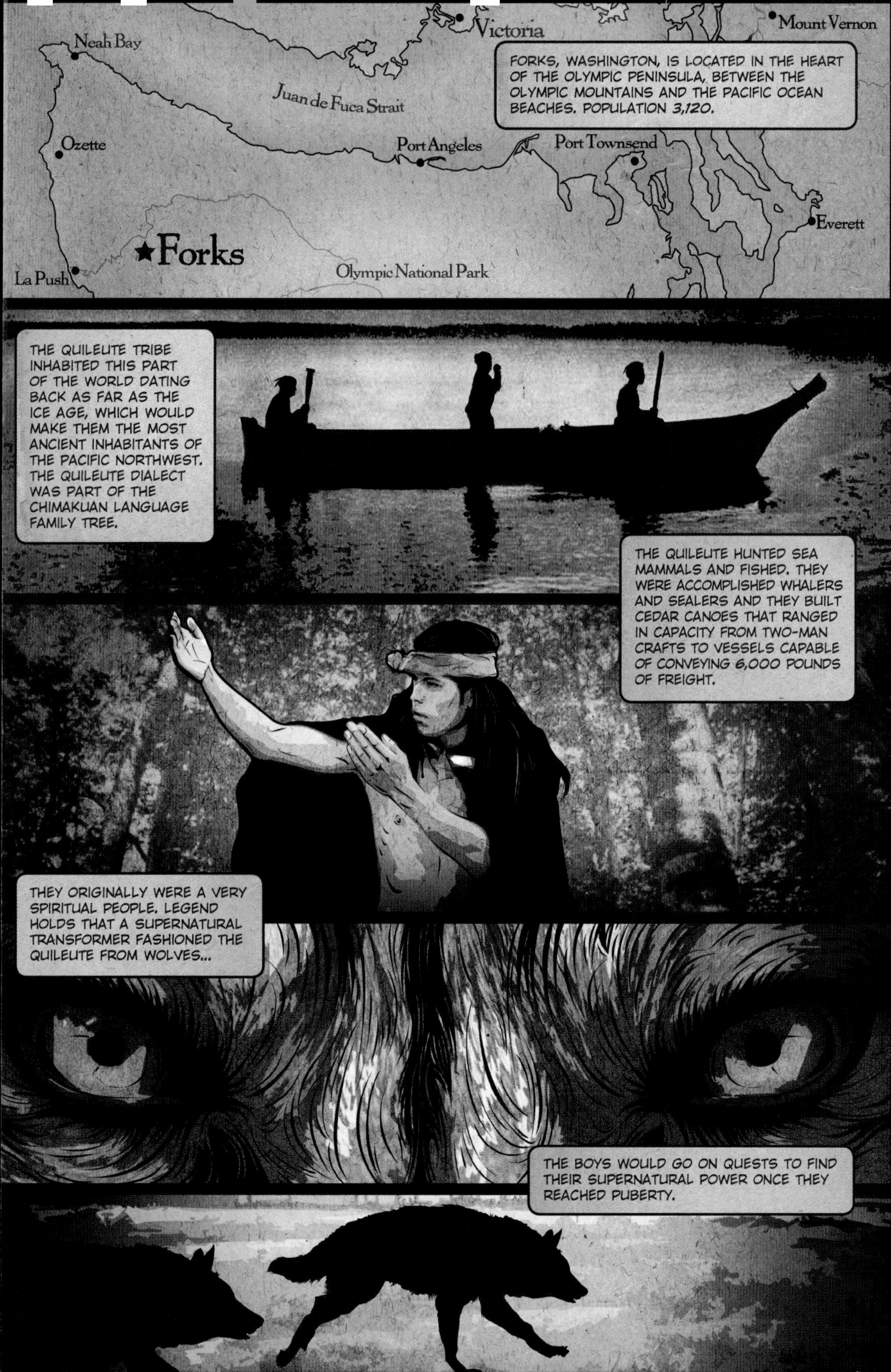

Victoria
Mount Vernon
Neah Bay
FORKS, WASHINGTON, IS LOCATED IN THE HEART OF THE OLYMPIC PENINSULA, BETWEEN THE OLYMPIC MOUNTAINS AND THE PACIFIC OCEAN BEACHES. POPULATION 3,120.
Juan de Fuca Strait
Ozette
Port Angeles
Port Townsend
Everett
Forks
La Push
Olympic National Park
THE QUILEUTE TRIBE INHABITED THIS PART OF THE WORLD DATING BACK AS FAR AS THE ICE AGE, WHICH WOULD MAKE THEM THE MOST ANCIENT INHABITANTS OF THE PACIFIC NORTHWEST. THE QUILEUTE DIALECT WAS PART OF THE CHIMAKUAN LANGUAGE FAMILY TREE.
THE QUILEUTE HUNTED SEA MAMMALS AND FISHED. THEY WERE ACCOMPLISHED WHALERS AND SEALERS AND THEY BUILT CEDAR CANOES THAT RANGED IN CAPACITY FROM TWO-MAN CRAFTS TO VESSELS CAPABLE OF CONVEYING 6,000 POUNDS OF FREIGHT.
THEY ORIGINALLY WERE A VERY SPIRITUAL PEOPLE. LEGEND HOLDS THAT A SUPERNATURAL TRANSFORMER FASHIONED THE QUILEUTE FROM WOLVES...
THE BOYS WOULD GO ON QUESTS TO FIND THEIR SUPERNATURAL POWER ONCE THEY REACHED PUBERTY.

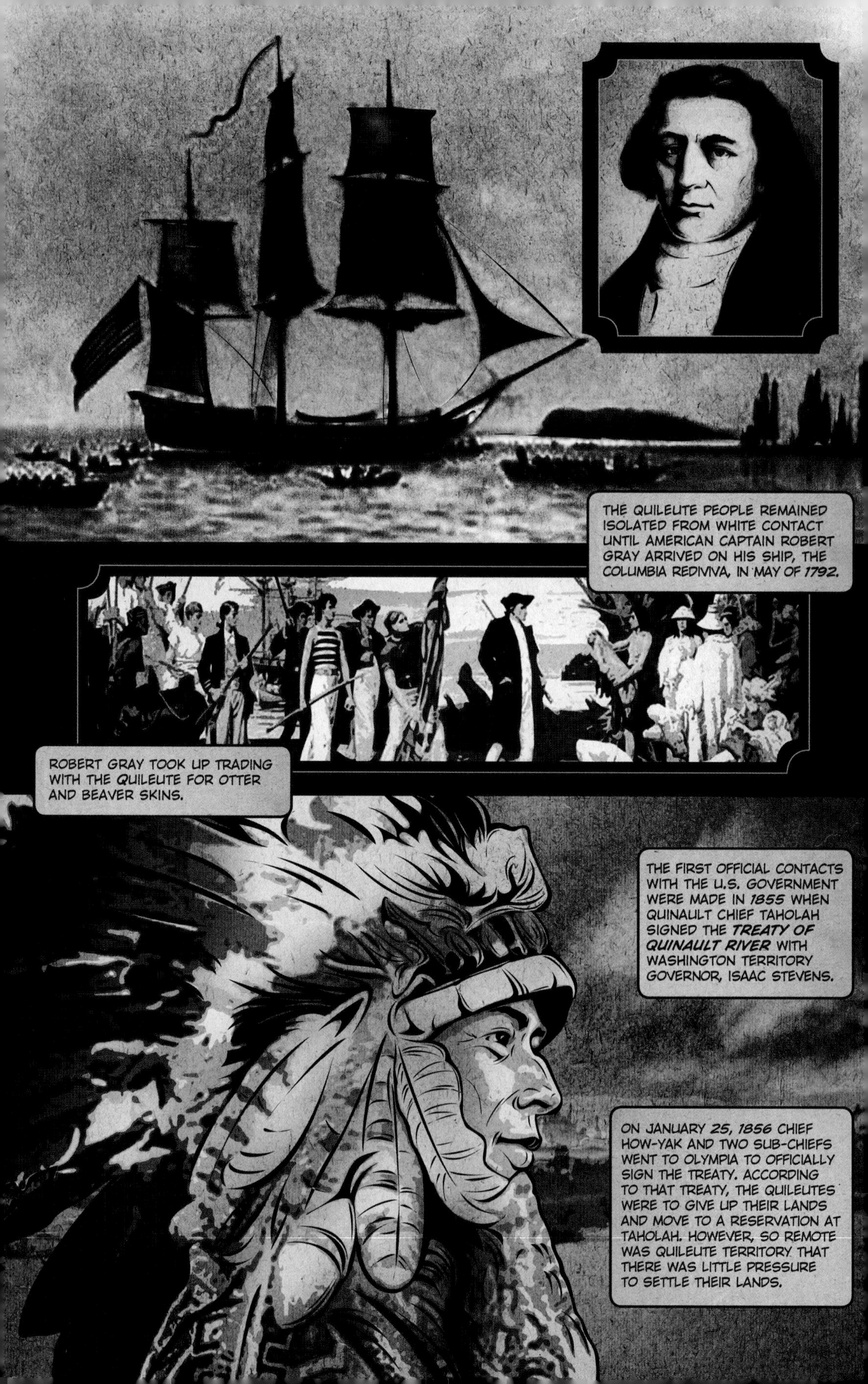
THE QUILEUTE PEOPLE REMAINED ISOLATED FROM WHITE CONTACT UNTIL AMERICAN CAPTAIN ROBERT GRAY ARRIVED ON HIS SHIP, THE COLUMBIA REDIVIVA, IN MAY OF 1792.
ROBERT GRAY TOOK UP TRADING WITH THE QUILEUTE FOR OTTER AND BEAVER SKINS.
THE FIRST OFFICIAL CONTACTS WITH THE U.S. GOVERNMENT WERE MADE IN 1855 WHEN QUINAULT CHIEF TAHOLAH SIGNED THE TREATY OF QUINAULT RIVER WITH WASHINGTON TERRITORY GOVERNOR, ISAAC STEVENS.
ON JANUARY 25, 1856 CHIEF HOW-YAK AND TWO SUB-CHIEFS WENT TO OLYMPIA TO OFFICIALLY SIGN THE TREATY. ACCORDING TO THAT TREATY, THE QUILEUTES WERE TO GIVE UP THEIR LANDS AND MOVE TO A RESERVATION AT TAHOLAH. HOWEVER, SO REMOTE WAS QUILEUTE TERRITORY THAT THERE WAS LITTLE PRESSURE TO SETTLE THEIR LANDS.

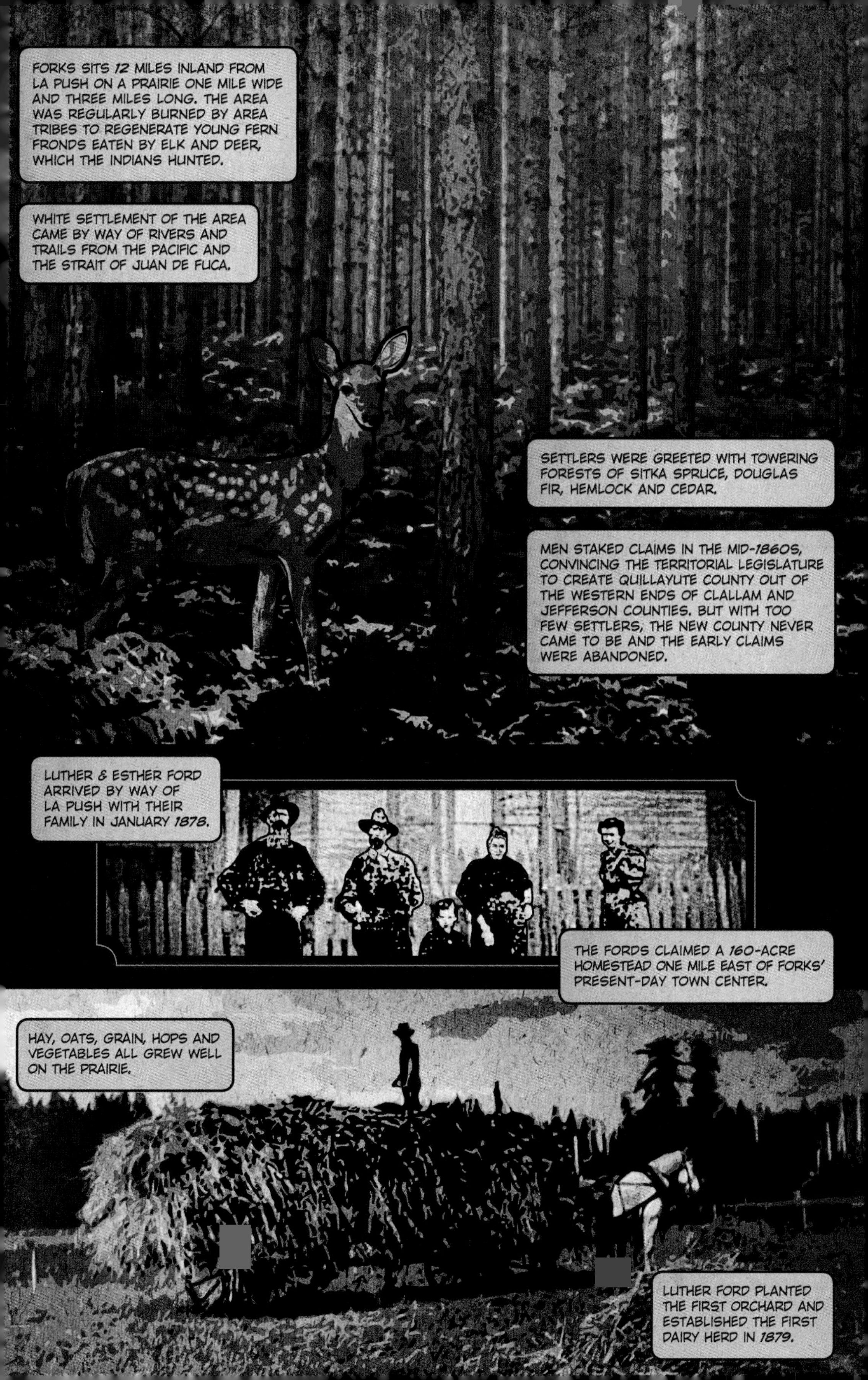
FORKS SITS 12 MILES INLAND FROM LA PUSH ON A PRAIRIE ONE MILE WIDE AND THREE MILES LONG. THE AREA WAS REGULARLY BURNED BY AREA TRIBES TO REGENERATE YOUNG FERN FRONDS EATEN BY ELK AND DEER, WHICH THE INDIANS HUNTED.
WHITE SETTLEMENT OF THE AREA CAME BY WAY OF RIVERS AND TRAILS FROM THE PACIFIC AND THE STRAIT OF JUAN DE FUCA.
SETTLERS WERE GREETED WITH TOWERING FORESTS OF SITKA SPRUCE, DOUGLAS FIR, HEMLOCK AND CEDAR.
MEN STAKED CLAIMS IN THE MID-1860S, CONVINCING THE TERRITORIAL LEGISLATURE TO CREATE QUILLAYUTE COUNTY OUT OF THE WESTERN ENDS OF CLALLAM AND JEFFERSON COUNTIES. BUT WITH TOO FEW SETTLERS, THE NEW COUNTY NEVER CAME TO BE AND THE EARLY CLAIMS WERE ABANDONED.
LUTHER & ESTHER FORD ARRIVED BY WAY OF LA PUSH WITH THEIR FAMILY IN JANUARY 1878.
THE FORDS CLAIMED A 160-ACRE HOMESTEAD ONE MILE EAST OF FORKS' PRESENT-DAY TOWN CENTER.
HAY, OATS, GRAIN, HOPS AND VEGETABLES ALL GREW WELL ON THE PRAIRIE.
LUTHER FORD PLANTED THE FIRST ORCHARD AND ESTABLISHED THE FIRST DAIRY HERD IN 1879.

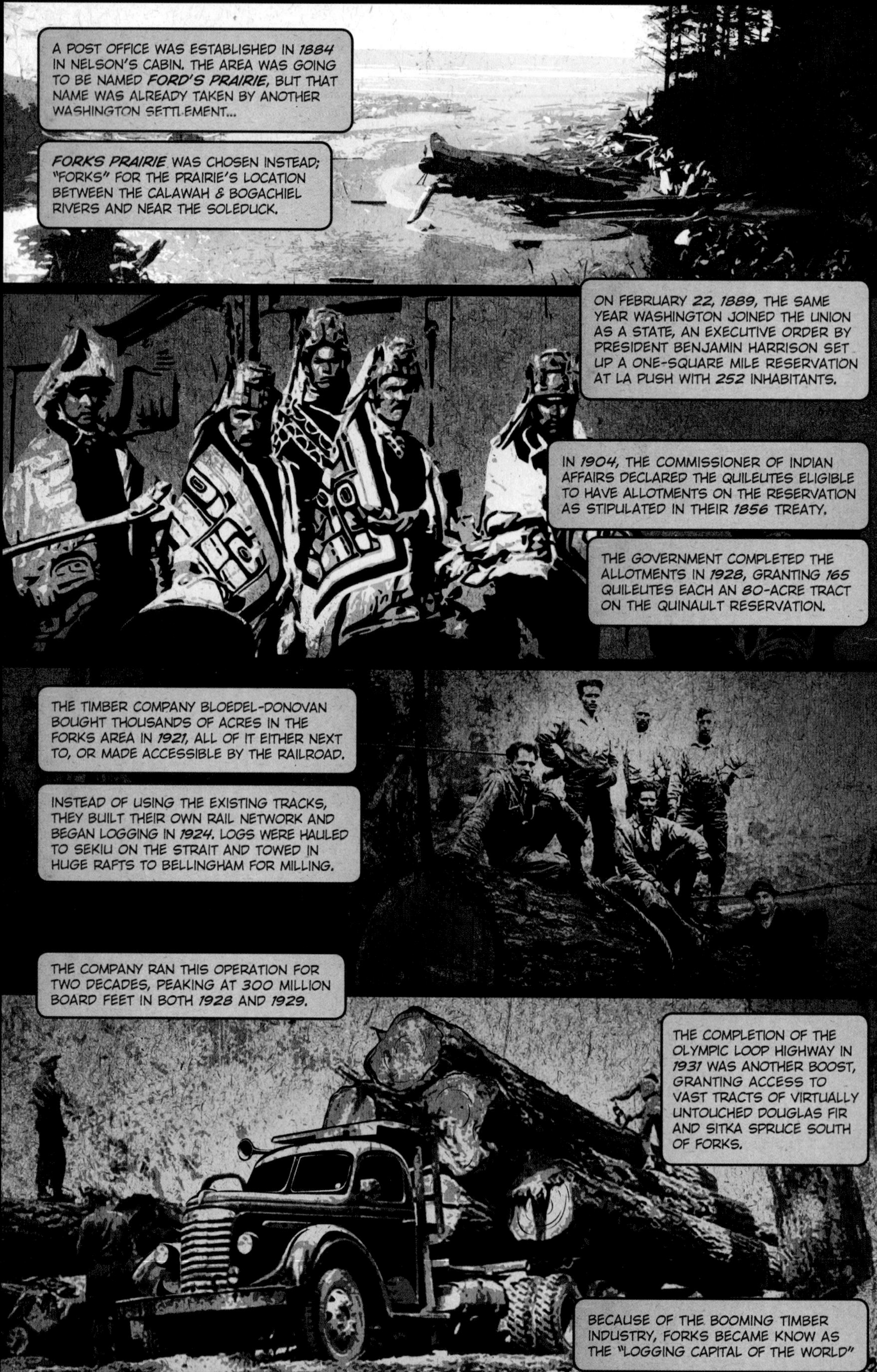
A POST OFFICE WAS ESTABLISHED IN 1884 IN NELSON'S CABIN. THE AREA WAS GOING TO BE NAMED FORD'S PRAIRIE, BUT THAT NAME WAS ALREADY TAKEN BY ANOTHER WASHINGTON SETTLEMENT...
FORKS PRAIRIE WAS CHOSEN INSTEAD; "FORKS" FOR THE PRAIRIE'S LOCATION BETWEEN THE CALAWAH & BOGACHIEL RIVERS AND NEAR THE SOLEDUCK.
ON FEBRUARY 22, 1889, THE SAME YEAR WASHINGTON JOINED THE UNION AS A STATE, AN EXECUTIVE ORDER BY PRESIDENT BENJAMIN HARRISON SET UP A ONE-SQUARE MILE RESERVATION AT LA PUSH WITH 252 INHABITANTS.
IN 1904, THE COMMISSIONER OF INDIAN AFFAIRS DECLARED THE QUILEUTES ELIGIBLE TO HAVE ALLOTMENTS ON THE RESERVATION AS STIPULATED IN THEIR 1856 TREATY.
THE GOVERNMENT COMPLETED THE ALLOTMENTS IN 1928, GRANTING 165 QUILEUTES EACH AN 80-ACRE TRACT ON THE QUINAULT RESERVATION.
THE TIMBER COMPANY BLOEDEL-DONOVAN BOUGHT THOUSANDS OF ACRES IN THE FORKS AREA IN 1921, ALL OF IT EITHER NEXT TO, OR MADE ACCESSIBLE BY THE RAILROAD.
INSTEAD OF USING THE EXISTING TRACKS, THEY BUILT THEIR OWN RAIL NETWORK AND BEGAN LOGGING IN 1924. LOGS WERE HAULED TO SEKIU ON THE STRAIT AND TOWED IN HUGE RAFTS TO BELLINGHAM FOR MILLING.
THE COMPANY RAN THIS OPERATION FOR TWO DECADES, PEAKING AT 300 MILLION BOARD FEET IN BOTH 1928 AND 1929.
THE COMPLETION OF THE OLYMPIC LOOP HIGHWAY IN 1931 WAS ANOTHER BOOST, GRANTING ACCESS TO VAST TRACTS OF VIRTUALLY UNTOUCHED DOUGLAS FIR AND SITKA SPRUCE SOUTH OF FORKS.
BECAUSE OF THE BOOMING TIMBER INDUSTRY, FORKS BECAME KNOW AS THE "LOGGING CAPITAL OF THE WORLD"

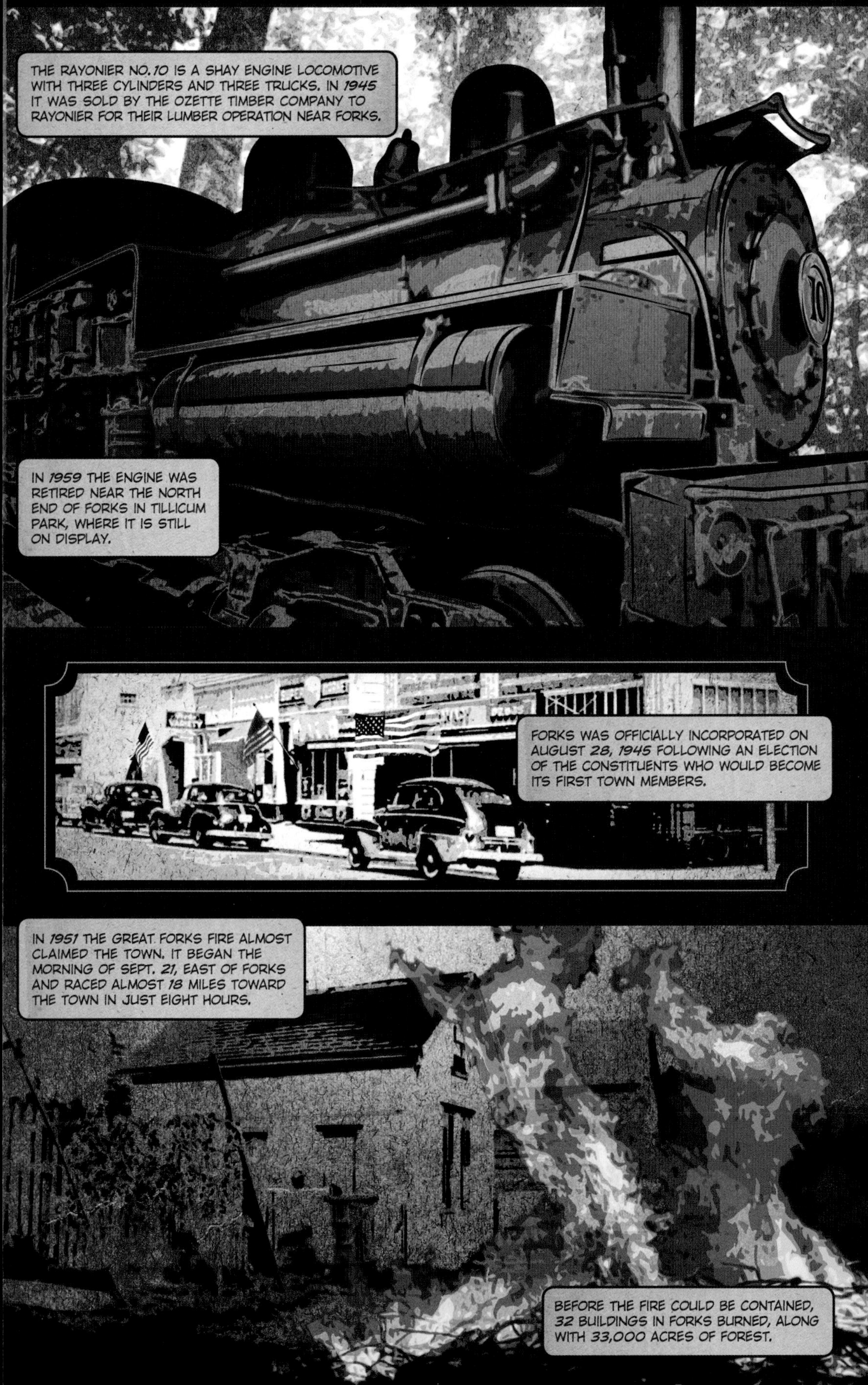
THE RAYONIER NO. 10 IS A SHAY ENGINE LOCOMOTIVE WITH THREE CYLINDERS AND THREE TRUCKS. IN 1945 IT WAS SOLD BY THE OZETTE TIMBER COMPANY TO RAYONIER FOR THEIR LUMBER OPERATION NEAR FORKS.
IN 1959 THE ENGINE WAS RETIRED NEAR THE NORTH END OF FORKS IN TILLICUM PARK, WHERE IT IS STILL ON DISPLAY.
FORKS WAS OFFICIALLY INCORPORATED ON AUGUST 28, 1945 FOLLOWING AN ELECTION OF THE CONSTITUENTS WHO WOULD BECOME ITS FIRST TOWN MEMBERS.
IN 1951 THE GREAT FORKS FIRE ALMOST CLAIMED THE TOWN. IT BEGAN THE MORNING OF SEPT. 21, EAST OF FORKS AND RACED ALMOST 18 MILES TOWARD THE TOWN IN JUST EIGHT HOURS.
BEFORE THE FIRE COULD BE CONTAINED, 32 BUILDINGS IN FORKS BURNED, ALONG WITH 33,000 ACRES OF FOREST.

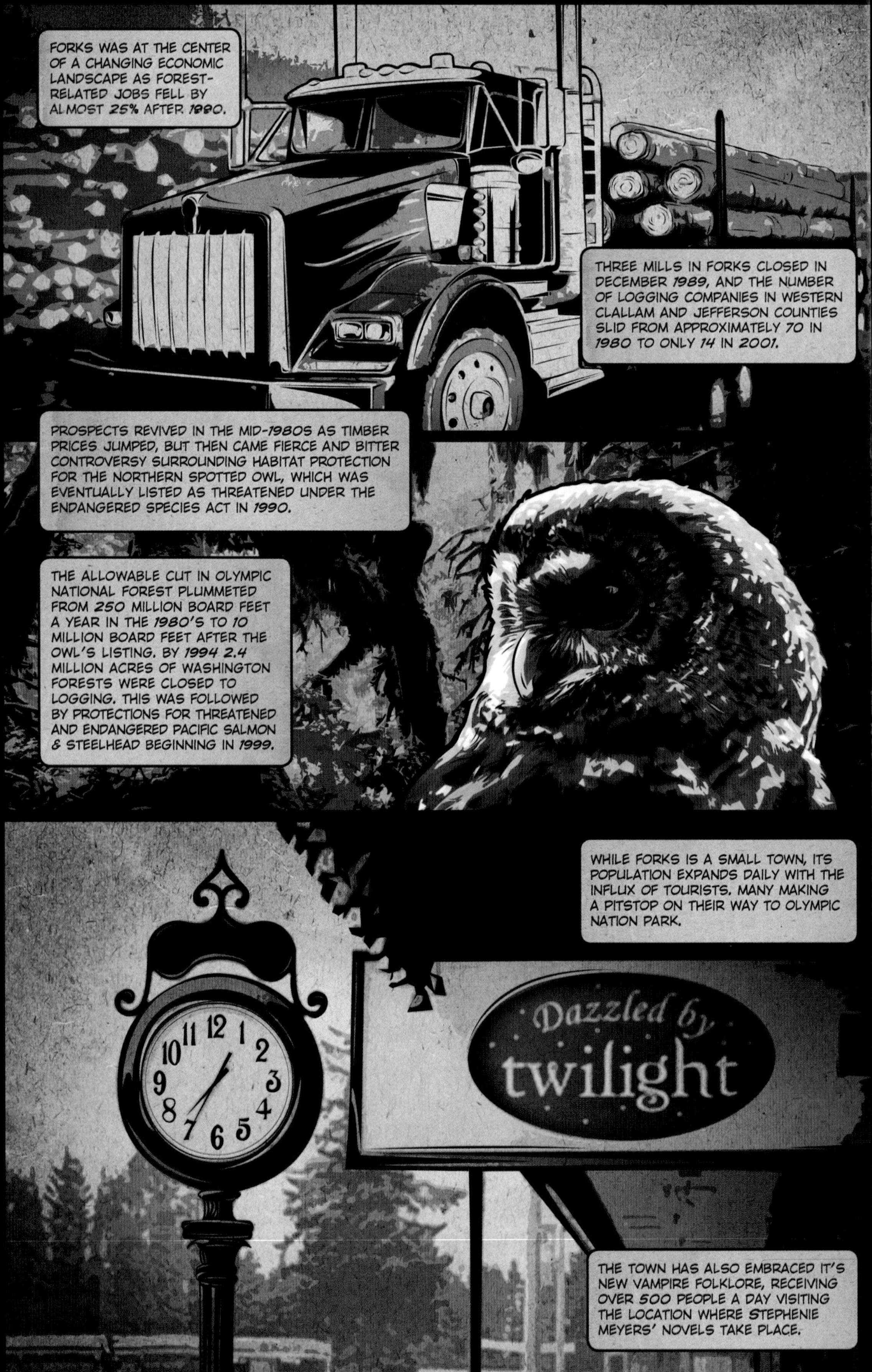
FORKS WAS AT THE CENTER OF A CHANGING ECONOMIC LANDSCAPE AS FOREST-RELATED JOBS FELL BY ALMOST 25% AFTER 1980.
THREE MILLS IN FORKS CLOSED IN DECEMBER 1989, AND THE NUMBER OF LOGGING COMPANIES IN WESTERN CLALLAM AND JEFFERSON COUNTIES SLID FROM APPROXIMATELY 70 IN 1980 TO ONLY 14 IN 2001.
PROSPECTS REVIVED IN THE MID-1980S AS TIMBER PRICES JUMPED, BUT THEN CAME FIERCE AND BITTER CONTROVERSY SURROUNDING HABITAT PROTECTION FOR THE NORTHERN SPOTTED OWL, WHICH WAS EVENTUALLY LISTED AS THREATENED UNDER THE ENDANGERED SPECIES ACT IN 1990.
THE ALLOWABLE CUT IN OLYMPIC NATIONAL FOREST PLUMMETED FROM 250 MILLION BOARD FEET A YEAR IN THE 1980'S TO 10 MILLION BOARD FEET AFTER THE OWL'S LISTING. BY 1994 2.4 MILLION ACRES OF WASHINGTON FORESTS WERE CLOSED TO LOGGING. THIS WAS FOLLOWED BY PROTECTIONS FOR THREATENED AND ENDANGERED PACIFIC SALMON & STEELHEAD BEGINNING IN 1999.
WHILE FORKS IS A SMALL TOWN, ITS POPULATION EXPANDS DAILY WITH THE INFLUX OF TOURISTS. MANY MAKING A PITSTOP ON THEIR WAY TO OLYMPIC NATION PARK.
Dazzled by twilight
THE TOWN HAS ALSO EMBRACED IT'S NEW VAMPIRE FOLKLORE, RECEIVING OVER 500 PEOPLE A DAY VISITING THE LOCATION WHERE STEPHENIE MEYERS' NOVELS TAKE PLACE.

Welcome to Forks

The Bluewater team took a field trip to Forks, the setting of Stephenie Meyer's Twilight saga. As you can see this picturesque town of 3200 residents on Washington's Olympic Peninsula has truly embraced the "spirit" of the books and films.

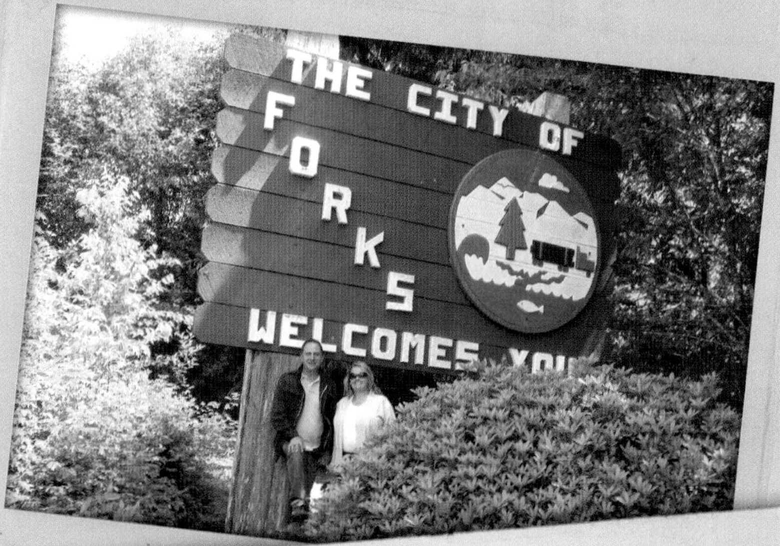
THE CITY OF
FORKS
WELCOMES YOU

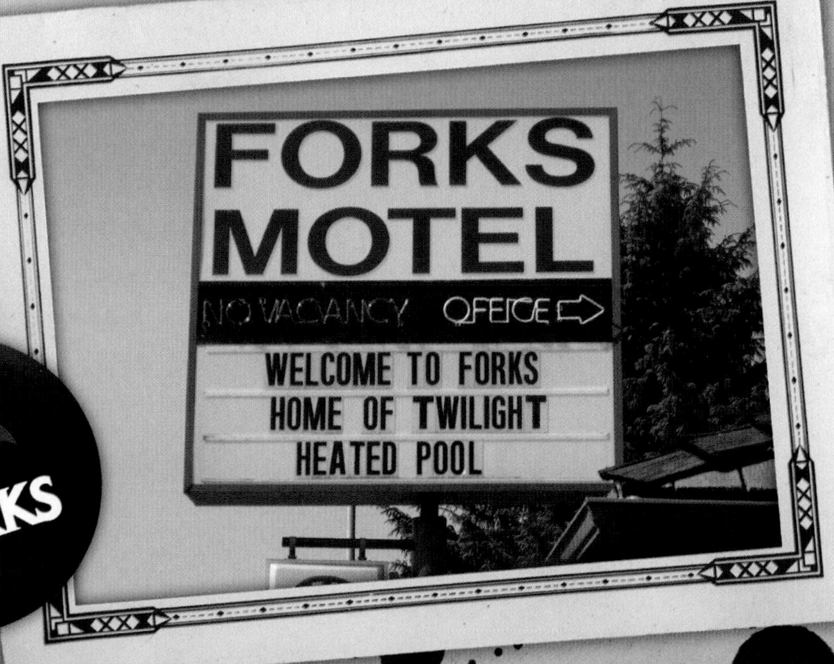
FORKS
MOTEL
NO VACANCY
OFFICE
WELCOME TO FORKS
HOME OF TWILIGHT
HEATED POOL

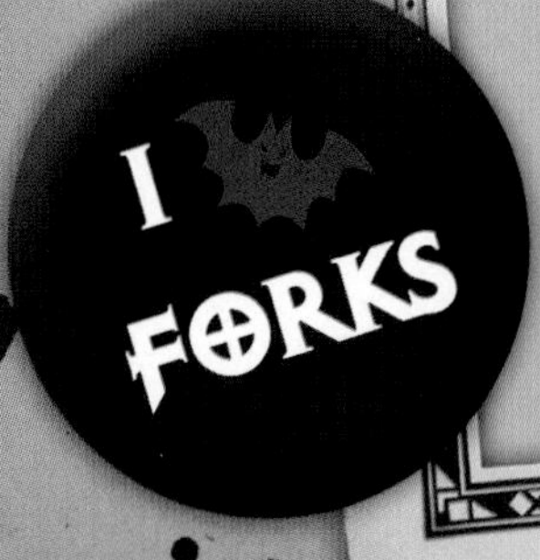
I
FORKS

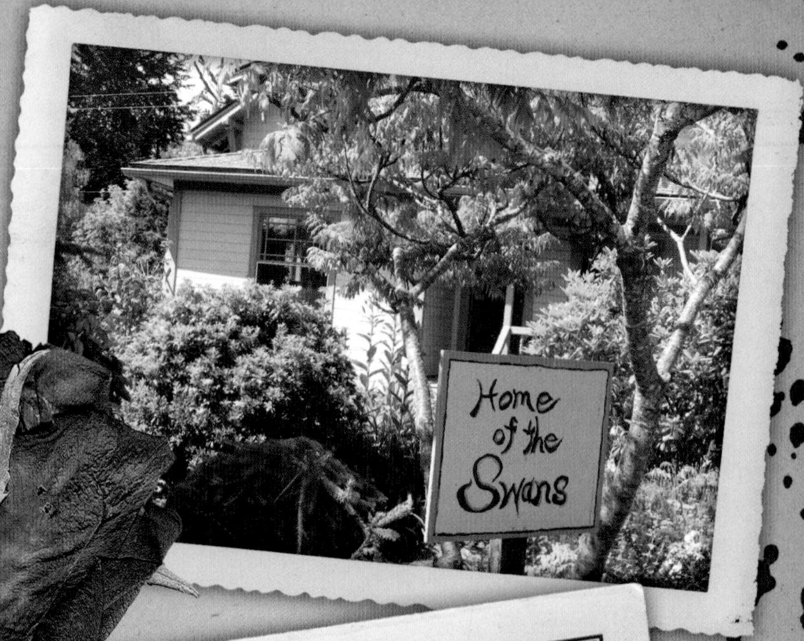
Home of the Swans

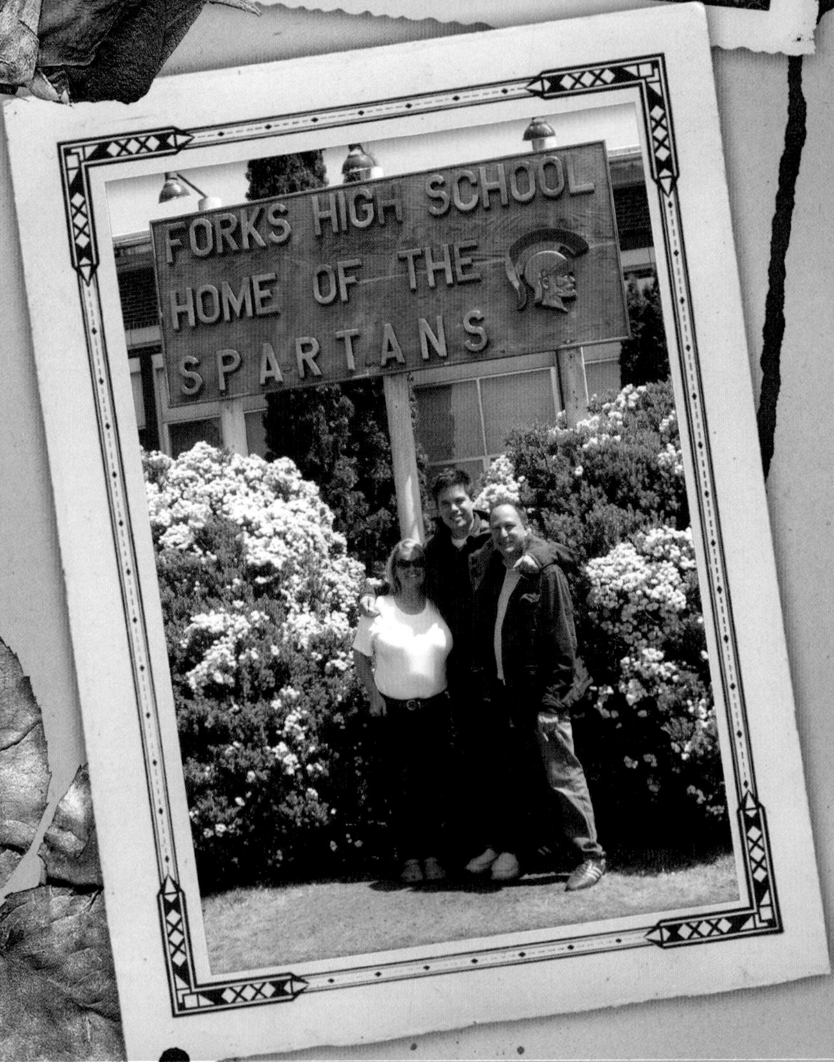
FORKS HIGH SCHOOL
HOME OF THE
SPARTANS

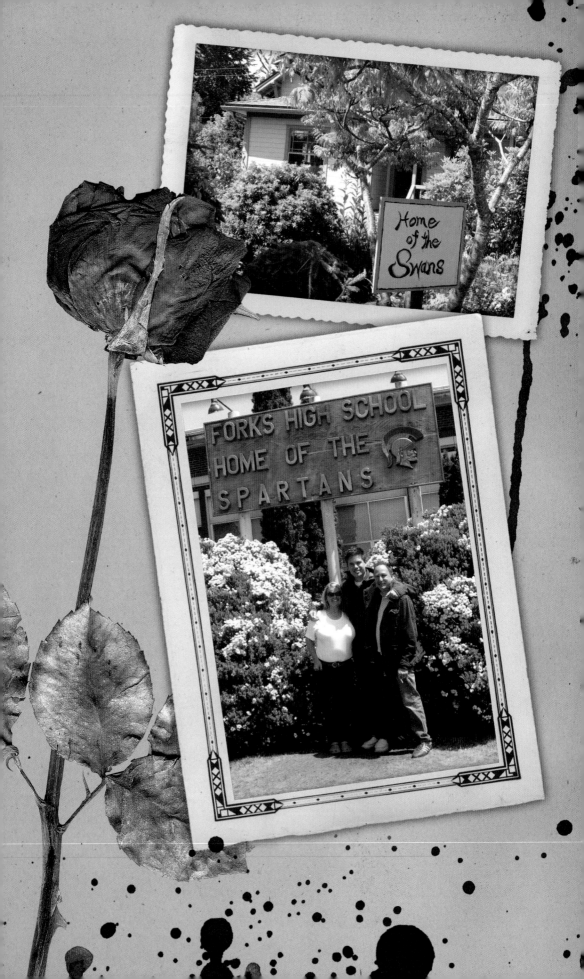

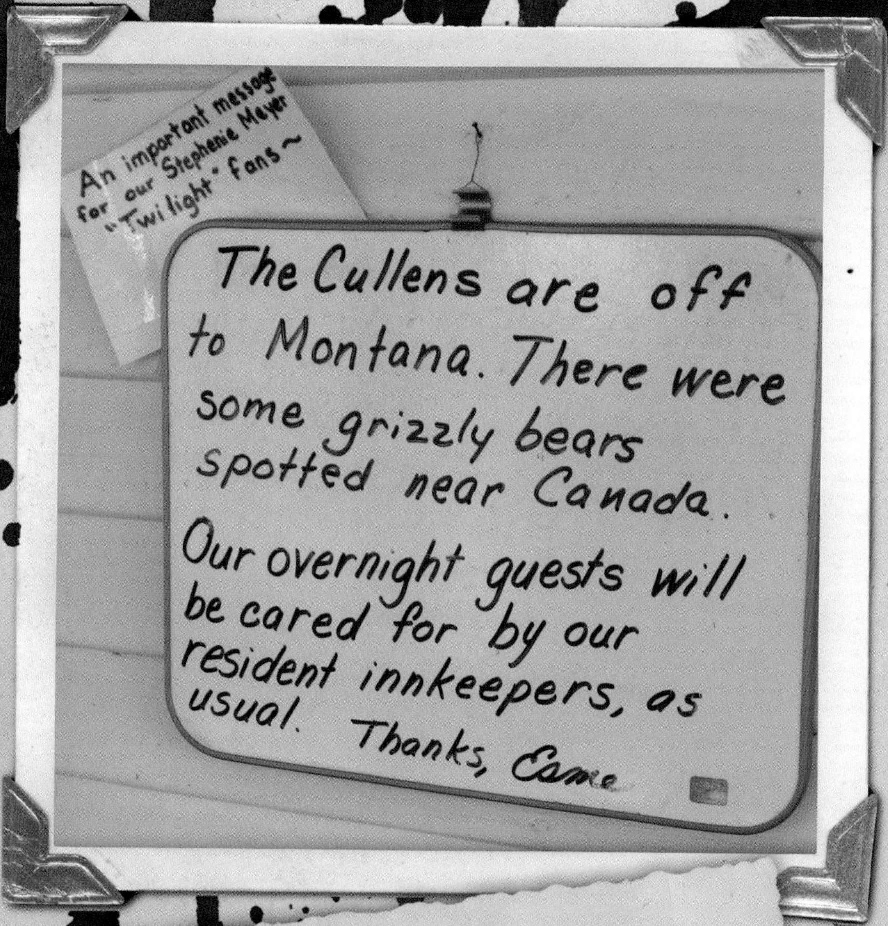
An important message
for our Stephenie Meyer
"Twilight" fans~
The Cullens are off
to Montana. There were
some grizzly bears
spotted near Canada.
Our overnight guests will
be cared for by our
resident innkeepers, as
usual. Thanks, Carrie

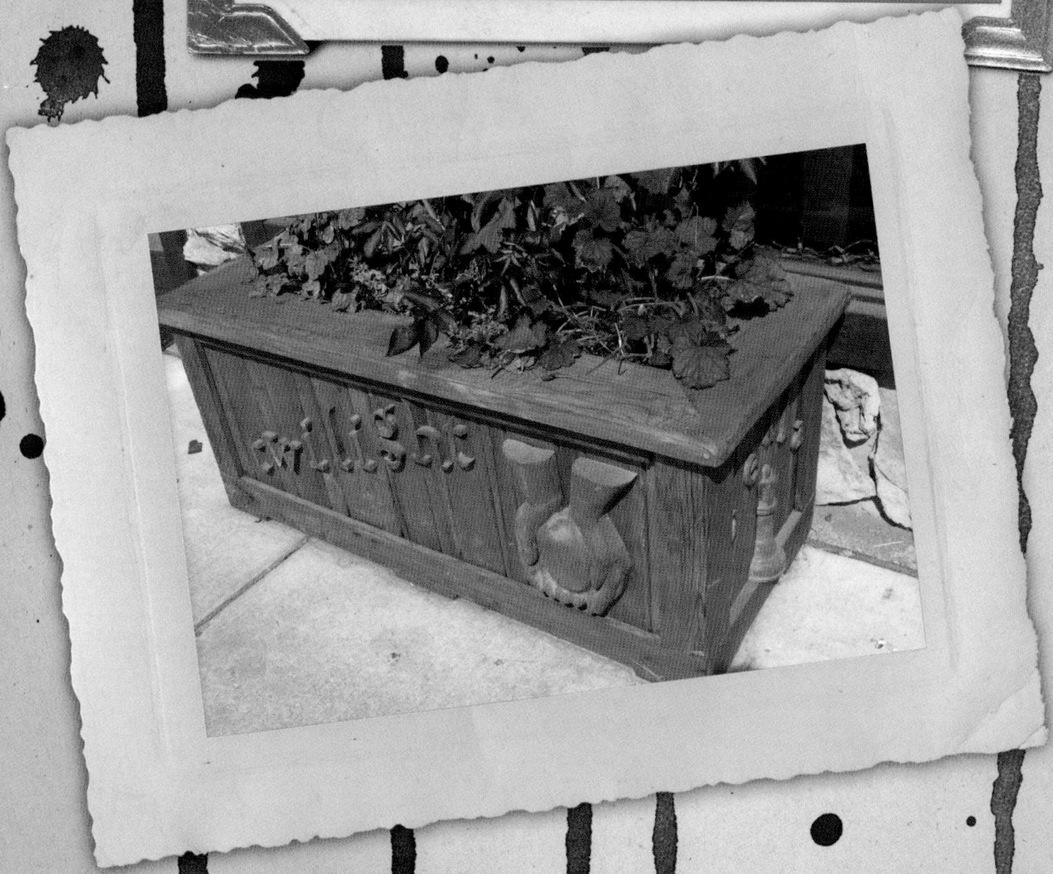

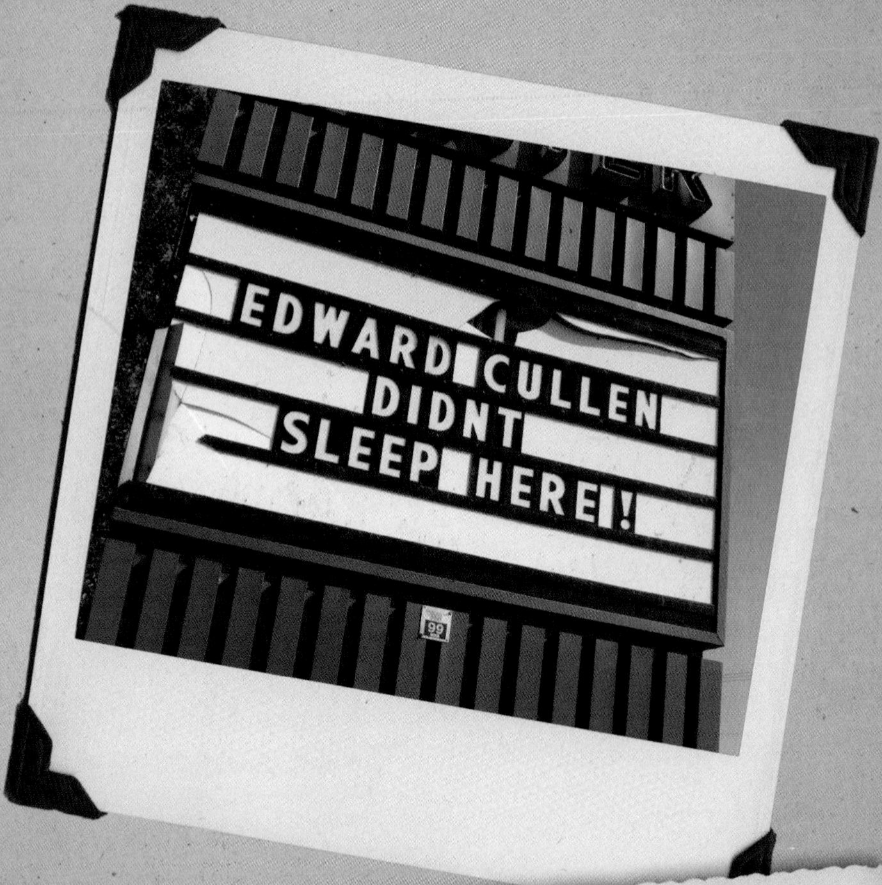
EDWARD CULLEN
DIDNT
SLEEP HERE!

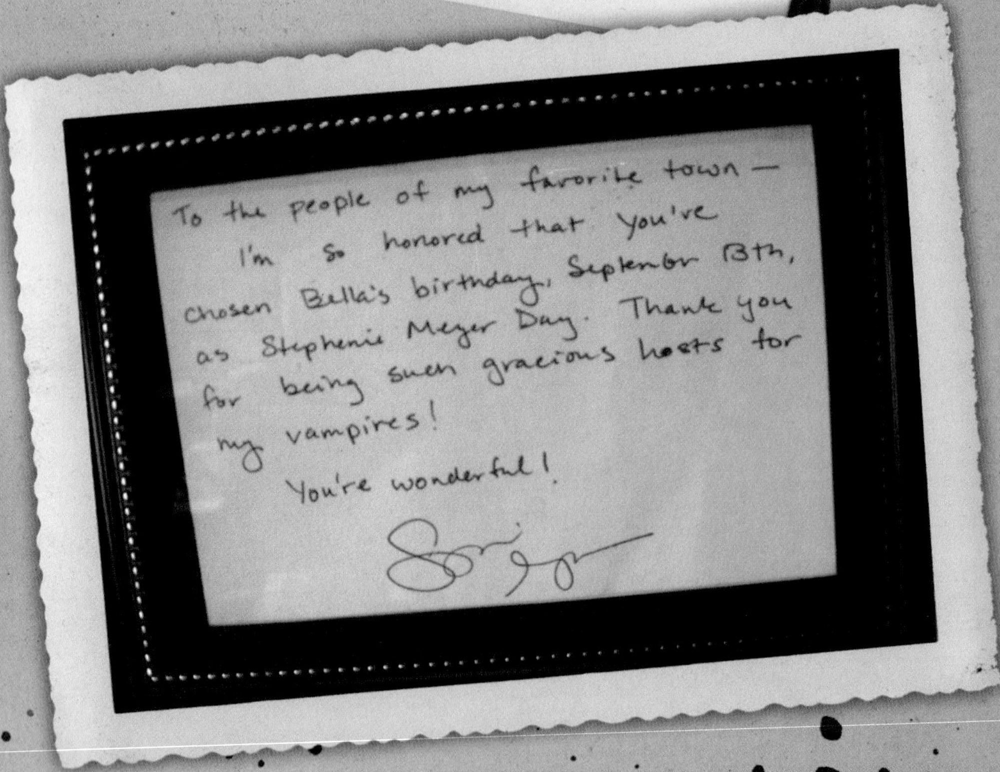
To the people of my favorite town—
I'm so honored that you've
chosen Bella's birthday, September 13th,
as Stephenie Meyer Day. Thank you
for being such gracious hosts for
my vampires!

You're wonderful!